PRINCESS OF THORNS AND RUIN

A VAMPIRE ROMANCE

THRONE OF SHADOWS
BOOK ONE

ANYA J COSGROVE

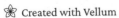

"If We Could Live Without Passion, Maybe We'd Truly Know Some Kind Of Peace. But We Would Be Hollow. Empty Rooms, Shuttered, And Dank. Without Passion, We'd Truly Be Dead."

Angelus, Buffy the Vampire Slayer

PLAYLIST

Castle - Halsey
You should see me in a crown - Billie Eilish
Pardon Me - Incubus
Beneath your Beautiful - Labrinth
Won't Stand Down - Muse
Black Black Heart - David Usher

CHAPTER 1

A DARK ROSE

ARIELLE

Blue-crested waves crash against the deadly cliffs below, and birds yap overhead. The sun shines a little harder the day before you die.

Lucas plucks the digital thermometer from my mouth, his red eyes sparkling. "35.4 degrees Celsius. Right on schedule."

Frosty patches bloom across my chest, and I rub my arms, hoping for even a touch of warmth from the friction. "I wish I didn't feel so cold."

The young vampire leans on the midnight-blue cushion at his back. An elusive smile plays with his lips like he's privy to an age-old secret he can't quite share with me, yet. "Don't worry, Ari. It won't be long now. A couple of days at most."

The vibrant Aegean Sea twinkles behind him, its swift, ever-changing currents mirroring my excitement.

"In a few days, we'll trade the olive trees and lazy mornings by the sea for the whirlwind of court." A pang of nostalgia tightens my chest, but it's quickly chased away by the thrill of impending change. It's been years since I've been home, since I've seen my brother, my cousins—my people.

Nothing happens here on the beautiful island of Hadria. The sun shines, the flowers offer bloom after bloom, and I'm bored. For three years, I studied, refined my skills, and not-so-patiently awaited my Nightfall ceremony—as it is customary for a woman of my rank.

I lay back on the chaise lounge and adjust the straps of my black swimsuit.

Lucas glances in my direction. "Careful. Your skin is changing, too. You don't want to catch a bad sunburn."

The way his gaze drags across my belly sends a shiver up my spine.

"But it melts the cold."

Lucas grins from the shade. "Enjoy it while you still can."

Nightfall comes between our sixteenth and twentieth birthday. I'm a late bloomer, but the cold death has finally arrived.

First, the drop in temperature.

Second, the aversion to sunlight.

Third, the thirst.

They say it burns as bright as lava and stings like a scorpion. They say the luscious taste of blood will threaten my sanity. But I'm ready to conquer it. If I don't, I'll be killed. Blood-crazed beasts, especially royals, are too dangerous to be left alive. I don't worry about it too much, though. I'm a Delacroix, a dark rose, a princess of night. The women in my family all survive their Nightfall.

Lucas stayed after his transition and waited for me, even though the sun now makes him squirm. He probably wasn't too keen to travel north during the winter anyway. He scratches a few notes on his acoustic guitar, and I close my eyes. His breath hitches when I start to sing. We've been friends for ten years, but lately, I've noticed a change.

He can't tear his gaze away, especially when I'm laughing or singing.

I crack one eye open discreetly. As I predicted, his clear red eyes are fixed on me. Long fingers fly across the strings, and I wonder what it would feel like if he touched me. Not brushed my shoulder or offered me his arm—I mean really touched me. If he knotted those fingers in my hair and crushed his mouth to mine, would it feel as good as I've imagined?

A fierce blush creeps up my chest. For a moment, I no longer feel cold. Between his dark brown curls, defined cheekbones, and the new, mesmerizing ridges of his stomach, my best friend has grown handsome. But none of it matters because he's not for me.

"Princess, the royal envoy is here," my handmaiden says with a quick curtsy.

"Thank you, Selene. Show her into my rooms. I'll be right there."

She turns to Lucas. "Do you need anything, my lord?"

He sets down his guitar with such care that I shiver, about ready to take its place across his lap.

"Please tell Quentin that I'll lunch in my room."

Selene nods and hurries back up the steps, her leather sandals brushing on the paved stones.

Lucas' smile doesn't quite reach his eyes. "I guess it's time."

"It's a good thing, Lucas." I rise to my feet and wrap my robe around my frame as he peels himself from his seat and pulls a white scarf over his face.

We climb back up to the small castle tucked on top of the cliff, and my heart pangs. I certainly won't be able to swim in the sea as much. I love the feel of salted water, but maybe this will change, too? I hope not.

Once we reach the gardens, Lucas veers toward his room, and I follow Selene to the front of the estate. An elderly woman waits for me in the shade of the entrance hall, her silhouette rattling my heart with its familiarity. Deep lines crease her face, her skin shriveled and dry.

She opens her arms wide. "Arielle, *ma princesse*. You've changed so much! Your beauty will blind the court. *Dieu*, your mother should have seen this day with her own eyes."

"Genevieve, how good it is to see you." I refrain from blinking so the tears won't spill over my lids. Princesses don't cry.

She cups my cheeks, an act that will be forbidden in only a few days—when I'm no longer a child, but a demon meant to hunt her kind. "How glad I am that I lived long enough to see this. I'll oversee your Nightfall, dear. Don't worry about a thing. The ceremony will be *grandiose*. Arranging it will be my last duty as your mother's first-blood."

I nod, not trusting my voice.

Genevieve hooks her arms around mine and ushers me along the gardens. "Have you decided if you want a man or a woman?"

I graze the roses with my fingertips. The white petals are soft to the touch, and a few of them fall to the ground in my wake. "I can't make up my mind. I've asked the Bringer to prepare an *échantillon* so I can meet a wide array of candidates."

"That's quite smart. You'll know when the time comes. Don't worry." She squeezes my arm.

How can I not worry? It's the most important decision of my life. One of the few I get to make by myself.

"How's Victor?" I ask, enquiring about my older brother, the king.

My *only* brother now, in fact.

"The whole court is still in shock over Ludovic's untimely death," Genevieve says with a frown.

My oldest brother, Ludovic, was killed a few weeks ago. He was two-hundred years old but expected to rule for many centuries. To humans, we're just annoyingly rich and powerful, but to demons, we're force of law. As the strongest breed of demons, we rule over the Shadow World and uphold our sacred laws.

"I'm glad Victor gets to be king. He might actually change things for the better," I say.

The starkness in Genevieve's gaze gives me pause.

"Victor will not rule as Ludovic did," I insist.

"Power changes people, Arielle. And not often for the better."

I don't like her tone one bit. She shouldn't be talking about Victor this way, and I open my mouth to reprimand her, but the child inside

5

me blushes at the prospect. "Will I be home in time for the corona-tion?" It's customary for a new king to wait ten to thirteen days before he's anointed.

"Yes. The government will hold a vote tomorrow to confirm your brother as heir, but it's only a formality since Ludovic had no chil-dren. The coronation should take place a few days later, and by then, your Nightfall will be over."

A cold wave numbs the tips of my fingers, and I hold my hand out to the bright sunshine but feel colder still. "Yes, it won't be long, now."

Tomorrow, the sun will go down, and I shall be reborn as a vampire.

CHAPTER 2
UNREQUITED
ARIELLE

The next morning, Genevieve joins me at the back of the reception hall. "Your mother was hiding in a similar corner when I met her."

The Bringer has thrown a lavish brunch in my honor, allowing me to meet my first-blood candidates.

First-bloods have an extremely important role to play in the life of a high-born vampire. Not only do they provide us with the blood we need to complete the transition, but they also become our human servants, sworn to feed and care for us for the rest of their lives. If we choose right, they can become our friends, confidantes, or counselors. Warm, dedicated lovers... Before old age and death claims them, that is.

Chandeliers twinkle above my head, and a thick flower garland hangs from the buffet table. The glorious menu includes salmon mousse, oysters, and free-flowing champagne, but I'm not hungry.

"It's so...loud," I say.

Genevieve chuckles. "You asked for a big sample. Twenty families sent a candidate."

I asked for a big sample because I have no idea who to choose.

Choosing a first-blood is a huge decision, the most important one I've had to make since I've been alive. As a princess, I don't get to make my own decisions often. I've been raised according to the standards of the night court and was brought to Hadria to await my Nightfall. I was a good student and perfected my knowledge of politics, geography, and etiquette. In Hadria, the villagers mostly veered out of my path. I've met a few locals, cut the ribbon when they inaugurated the new library, and appeared at a few banquets, but I've never really talked with normals. These humans live and breathe in a different world from us. They aren't serving the realm—or the dark Gods.

They know of vampires because they were born on the island, but most of them went to school on the continent, and the supernatural world is as intangible to them as the twenty-first century is to me.

Their discrete, half-terrified glances create trails of goosebumps that creep along my arms. Under their scrutiny, I'm an object of fascination more than a person. Very few candidates meet my gaze.

"I thought they'd be like the humans in the village, not so...glamorous and fidgety."

"They are nervous, princess. They have been awaiting this moment for years, hoping to be chosen. For some of them, it's their last chance to serve our family. You are the last royal transitioning until your cousin Janelle comes of age, and the little bloodling is only ten."

"Well, it's awkward." Since I can't keep lurking on the outskirts of my own party, I gulp down the rest of my mimosa, hand the empty flute to Genevieve, and roll my shoulders back. "Here goes."

Big, fashionable pockets flap on each side of my boat-neck cocktail dress as I walk. I sink my hands into them and stroll to the middle of the reception hall. The soft satin stops right above my knees and highlights what is sure to be my last tan.

A tall girl about my age stumbles at my approach, her blue eyes glued to my thick fishtail braid. "Wow. I mean—sorry. Wow. You're even more beautiful than they've said."

Heat spreads in my chest, and I find enough courage to free my hands from my pockets. "What's your name?"

"Leta."

Leta's eyes are level with mine, but her athletic body thickens her silhouette. Her red dress exposes her belly button and leaves one side of her stomach and her waist bare. A round metal ring holds the fabric in place at her hip, before it falls all the way to the floor. It's not my style, but it's gorgeous.

A fresh, flowery scent seeps into my nose as I walk closer. "How old are you, Leta?" The name rolls off my tongue naturally, which I take as a good sign.

"Eighteen."

"Young. That's good." She could serve me for many years, and her beauty will last for decades. "Why do you want to pledge your life to me?"

She blushes and opens her mouth, but no sound comes out.

The man standing next to her extends his hand in a business-like fashion. "Darin Ellis, your highness."

I shake it with a smirk. Shaking hands? What is this, a job interview? "Ellis. Right. You're related to Gregor Ellis, my brother's first-blood."

The man beams. A thick beard covers the bottom half of his face. "He's my great uncle, princess."

Bottom lip tucked between my teeth, I appraise him. "You look old."

He smiles, unfazed by the jab. "I'm 27."

"That's a bit old."

"Hey, I'm not the oldest." Darin nods to the other side of the room.

The oldest man in attendance—according to Darrin—has wild, dirty blond hair, the sides buzzed shorter than the top. His knees are slightly bent, and his broad shoulders hunch like he's trying to downplay his height and avoid attention.

I offer a polite nod to Darin and Leta. "Excuse me, I need to confer with my advisor."

Wide-eyed, they exchange a glance, and a hint of guilt colors my cheeks.

I hope they don't think that I've made up my mind already.

I find Genevieve in the crowd. The old human woman is munching on a fine cheese platter a few feet to my left, and I glide over to her.

"Who's that?" I ask, pointing to the older man.

She peeks into her planner. "Leopold Callas. Reputable family, but old. The Bringer made an exception about his age because the family's preferred candidate died unexpectedly last week. He lives on the mainland and booked his ferry ticket late last night."

The crowd parts for me as I make my way to him.

He's not like the men I know. He's...larger. His hands are twice the size of mine, and they look rough and used. Even though he's wearing a suit, he's not as clean-cut and pampered as the other candidates.

While his posture downplays his height, the color of his eyes steals my tongue. Green, lush irises meet my gaze before he bows his head. He must have shaved in a hurry because he missed a tiny spot underneath his jaw, the remnants of stubble visible. My fingers itch to reach for it, but I keep my arms firmly at my sides.

"Your highness." The greeting is both gruff and quiet.

"Are you hiding from me, Mr. Callas?" I ask with exaggerated solemness.

"Yes," he answers quickly.

I grin at his honesty. "You're not mingling. Or eating. Why?"

"I'm—" He closes his mouth and shakes his head. "It's all very intimidating." The wrinkled white undershirt clings to his skin, the edge of a tattoo visible beneath his collar.

The ink drawing tickles my curiosity, and I try to guess its shape, but too much of it disappears below the stuffy fabric. The day is particularly hot, and I bet Leopold is sweaty under that thick jacket of his—and I'm grateful for my light blue dress. He seems to be thinking the same thing, his eyes fixed on the hem of silk at my mid-thigh like he's curious to touch it. A strange energy sticks in the air, pulling me in.

"You're intimidated by me, Mr. Callas?" I slide closer and gaze up at him. Leather and musk caress my nose, along with a zest of citrus and the sting of a salty ocean breeze...

"You're a vampire princess," he says slowly, like he's reminding himself.

"Just a princess...for now." I bite back a grin. "My entourage told me you decided to show up for the ceremony on a whim. You booked your ferry ticket last-minute. Why?"

His shoulders move nervously under his jacket. "I'm 29, your majesty. I didn't think I had much of a chance." The deep rumbles of his Greek accent scatter goosebumps across my neck.

I raise a brow. "Why should I choose you? Since you're old and fickle?"

Leopold pushes himself off the wall, fire raging in his green eyes, and his voice is not timid nor servile when he answers, "I am *not* fickle."

A dizzying warmth blossoms in my chest, our eyes locked in a battle he certainly intends to win.

Another candidate approaches us from the side, his brows pulled together in stark disapproval. "You dare raise your voice to your princess, Callas?"

Leopold stiffens and bows his head again. "Pardon me, your highness."

I want to slap the newcomer for interrupting, but the strange energy has vanished, and Leopold keeps his gaze firmly planted on the ground. With a cold nod, I greet the new candidate.

"Princess, it's such an honor to meet you." The man has dark hair and an easy smile. "I'm Glenn Floyd." He's drop-dead gorgeous, too, with sharp gray eyes and a proud chin. "I'd love to see the gardens."

"Lead the way, Mr. Floyd." It's only fair to meet every candidate, and Mr. Callas certainly isn't eager to escort me through the gardens.

Glenn links his arm in mine and guides me under the big stone arch. Roses stick out of the bushes and graze his jacket as we weave along the path.

"It's your last stroll under the sun, princess."

A boulder pulses in my throat. "My last pleasant one. Tell me about yourself, Mr. Floyd."

We walk along the tortuous path while Glenn recounts all the wonderful things his family's accomplished, and his own many gifts. I find myself spacing out during most of the conversation, my mind occupied with the gravity of the decision I have to make in less than an hour.

My future, my legacy, my *happiness* hinges on this...vapid brunch.

When we round back to the buffet, Glenn kisses my pulse point, and while one part of me is flattered to receive the undivided attention of such a gorgeous man, another squirms at how rehearsed his manners feel.

I scan the bustling room. Dessert has been served, and the free-flowing alcohol loosened the candidates' tongues. Eager to please the Bringer for his efforts, I meet a dozen more of them.

Leta chats with Leopold with her back to me, the man's tall frame towering next to the champagne fountain. Our gazes meet over the tall pile of assorted macaroons, but he quickly turns away, fills his glass to the brim, and gulps it down.

My non-existent appetite leaves a hollow space in my belly, and while I'll continue to nimble on human food after tonight, I know my last brunch is behind me. Starting tomorrow, blood is going to count for most of my calories, supplied by one of these humans. One of these strangers will become my servant, and I'll feed on him—or her—every day.

"Did you make up your mind, *ma chérie*?" Genevieve asks.

A knot spools in my stomach. "Leta was nice. Bubbly. Ellis seems incredibly clever. Glenn is handsome—it's such a big decision to make in so little time."

"Trust your instincts. Blood is all about intuition. You're not shopping for a friend or a spouse. Your first-blood might make you laugh or offer advice, but those aren't his or her primary functions. You're looking for something deeper, a visceral connection that goes beyond small talk or physical attraction."

My ears heat up. "You mean to say that Glenn is cocky and slick, and that I should trust my gut?"

"Exactly." A strand of hair has come undone from my braid, and Genevieve tucks it behind my ear. Her colorful rings sparkle in the midday sun. "Nightfall is a sensitive time. You'll be very weak. You need to choose someone strong. Someone who's not afraid."

"Why should they be afraid? I intend to treat my first-blood well."

Genevieve pats my arm. "Very few of us die during the Nightfall, but some do, and the rare, unfortunate souls who mistakenly get turned into vampires aren't allowed to serve their patron. They are enrolled in the army instead, and you have to admit, that's a harsh fate. Whatever happens, they won't have a life of their own. No career, no family. You have to appreciate their sacrifice."

"I do." My tongue sticks to the roof of my mouth, parched and dry. Can I understand what these humans are going through? Probably not. If chosen, they'll be respected, but set apart. They'll lose their freedom and say my name ten times more a day than their own.

The thought soothes the ache in my belly. I don't need anyone to compliment me or sing my praises. I need a lifeline in this lonely royal existence, someone who won't be afraid to step on my toes and tell me the truth.

And there is only one voice in this reception hall that could make my traditional—and mostly boring name—sound interesting.

CHAPTER 3

REAPED

LEO

The Bringer, Jorge, smiles to the crowd and steps to the top of the staircase leading back inside the Delacroix estate. His thick gray beard reminds me of my dad as he spreads his arms in greeting. "You are to be praised for the way each of you conducted yourselves this morning. You do your families proud."

The side of my one-size-too-small, polished shoe scrapes the stone wall. I'm standing in the very back of the interior courtyard, hoping this concludes quickly. The shadow of the building offers a respite from the harsh afternoon sun, my sleeves rolled up to my elbows. With the heat and nerves, I'm sweaty as fuck. Zara must be worried sick, and about ready to kick my ass for coming here, but I had no other choice.

Jorge wets his lips and pries a tight scroll from the interior pocket of his stuffy jacket. He treats this ceremony with the seriousness and decorum that has been expected of him since he pledged his life to the Dark fucking King. He enjoys the show, the drama, the anticipation. Dad used to say that his brother had always been fascinated by evil. "Our princess has chosen her first-blood. The honor goes to..." The brittle piece of parchment creases in his big hands as he rolls it open, and his gaze darts to the ground. "Leopold Callas."

...

He didn't really call my name, did he?

I roll my shoulders back, certain I misunderstood. The heads of my *competitors* turn to me, and dark spots dance in front of my eyes.

"Come forward, Leo," Jorge says quietly.

In a haze, I push off the wall. The heavy sun beats my cheeks as the crowd parts for me, but I struggle to walk in a straight line, my vision eddied by a perverse kaleidoscope of colors. Blood pools in my chest, and my legs are stiff, but I walk forward until I reach the stairs and bow my head. This is a dream. A nightmare. I'm going to wake up.

I'm going to wake up.

I'm

going

to

wake

up.

Jorge hands me a sealed ceremonial scroll. "Congratulations. You have a few hours to say your goodbyes. Please report to me before six o'clock." He leans closer and whispers, "I never thought—"

"Thank you, sir." I turn on my heels.

The others pat me on the back, and chant my name in cheer. Most of them mean it, and I clench my fists not to punch the daylight out of them. Can't they see that my life is over? I'd gladly trade places with them, but it's too late.

I should never have come.

Why the hell did she choose me?

I talked back to her.

I made sure that Darin told her I was old. Too old.

Glenn Floyd had her wrapped around his sleazy fingers.

He looks glum, and the nasty pout on his face is the one, tiny positive thing about this hellish outcome. I hate the guy, and he wanted this. He was born to suck up to a vampire princess, and yet his disappointment is a slim consolation prize. My life is no longer mine. My dreams will never come true. My plans are nothing but ashes at my feet.

Why *the fuck* did she choose me?

How vain is it of me to find solace in his failure?

I drag my feet to the stacked, sun-battered houses perched at the top of the cliff. Their stark white exteriors contrast with the blue sky, and I can't tell where the houses end and the puffy clouds behind them begin.

When I rest my hand on my neighbor's cottage, a burst of heat engulfs me, thick and suffocating. Kit, the red tabby cat, mewls as he slithers between my legs.

Acid burns my throat, and I empty my stomach next to his front paws.

Kit arches his back and side steps to avoid most of the mess, his fur sticking out in all directions, before he scampers off. I swipe the back of my hand across my mouth and force a deep breath down my lungs.

Worst part is: Mum will be proud.

Zara's quick footsteps tread down the skewed alleyway. Cold sweat gathers at the back of my neck as I turn to face her, to stare at the sum of my broken promises.

Her long blond hair flows in the wind, her beautiful green eyes still puffy and red from the fight we had this morning.

She considers the barf on the step and stiffens as she approaches me. "You said you were too old... You said there was *no* chance."

"I'm sorry, Zara."

A strangled cry parts her lips, and she grips my forearm with more strength than I thought possible. "Let's run away." Her nails dig into my arm. "Now."

My heartbeat spikes off into a crazy-fast drum solo. "You know I can't. I have a duty to my family."

She beats my chest with her small fists. "I told you not to go. I told you any princess would notice you—"

I wish her punches would hurt more, but I can barely feel them, my entire body numb. "Mum gave up her scholarship—her whole future—for me when she was young. I couldn't let her die from that damn cancer."

"It's not your fault she got pregnant so young."

"She gave up everything for me once, and now it's my turn to sacrifice something for her. I didn't think she'd last another month, and now she will be cured by their warlocks. *Cured*, Zara. Just like that."

When my uncle told me he could get Mum a magical cure for her cancer in exchange for me representing the Callas family at the Delacroix choosing brunch, I didn't hesitate. The vampires reward the first-blood candidates largely, so most families consider it a great honor to just take part in the proceedings. I had almost no chance to be chosen, but I knew there was a chance. A tiny one.

I gambled my life away. Too bad I won't be around to see Mum healthy again.

"Mum will get a lifetime allowance, so she'll be taken care of. Everything I own is now yours. I'll arrange everything, I promise," I say, finally meeting her gaze to show her I mean it.

She bends forward like a broken doll, her hands on my shoulders, forehead touching my chest. "Don't go."

"It's too late now. We'd all be executed if I don't."

She glances over her shoulder and tugs on my arm. "Come to the house for a minute. We can figure this out—"

"Zara. Zara." I cup her face in my hands softly. "There's nothing to be done."

"Please Leo...I need to hold you. Touch you." The desperation in her voice mirrors my own, and her hand flies to the button of my jeans. She pulls my zipper down, but I grip her wrist to stop her.

"Stop. We're in the middle of the street."

"Then come with me." Between sniffles and pleading, her gaze hardens. "If all we have is an hour, then so be it, but don't be so cruel as to deny me that."

Chills snake along my spine, and my stomach cramps. "It's too hard... I can't face your family, or hide in your room for the rest of the day. I have to get all my stuff in order in mere hours. I can't afford to fall apart." I want to be considerate and help her through her grief, but the truth is, I'm too wrapped up in mine.

"You—you asshole! I told you not to go! I told you the princess would sink her dirty claws into you! You think I'm naive? I know what the men in town say about her. I know what you two will do together. I can't believe you chose a nineteen year old bimbo over me," she repeats the angry words from this morning, sounding like a broken record, but the more she lashes out, the more I retreat within myself, suddenly feeling exhausted and numb.

I can't believe she's implying that I traded my life in exchange for a good fuck.

The Bringer appears, turning the corner and heading in our direction. "Don't blame him, Miss Andreas," Jorge says. "The fault is mine." His gold sequin Bringer robe scratches the stones as I meet his guilty stare. "I never expected this, Leo."

"I know, uncle. But it happened." My knuckles itch, and like a man who lost everything at cards, I really, really wish I could punch the dealer and make it all go away.

Zara throws him a nasty glance and shouts, "Do something about it, then! Tell them you made a mistake. Tell the stupid undead bitch he's unfit for the role—"

"Enough!" Jorge clips, "If you don't stop speaking about our beloved princess in this manner, I'll have to arrest you."

The neighbor peers through the closest window, the commotion quickly attracting too much attention, and my heart hammers. "I need to warn Mum."

A dry sob quakes Zara's chest as she grips the front of my shirt. "Please, Leo. I can't bear the thought of losing you."

I can't... It's too much. "You'll find someone else."

She shakes her head, almost violently. "No, I won't!"

I firmly peel her hands away from my shirt and bring them up to my mouth. "Think of me as dead, Z." I whisper as I kiss her knuckles.

Tears stream down her round cheeks, and it kills me, but I walk away. I'll never see her again, the woman I planned to marry.

"Miss Andreas, let me escort you home." Jorge puts a comforting hand on her shoulder as he guides her back to her parents house, her uncontrollable sobs now shaking her entire body.

My soul in shambles, I enter the house where I was born through the kitchen. Mum glances up from her scrapbook, her frail hand curled over a cracked picture of my father, a large yellow hoodie hanging from her bones.

The human treatments left her without hair and skinny as fuck. I'm so glad that she won't have to endure anymore chemo. Jorge will provide the cure as soon as possible, and now that I've been chosen, I don't have to worry about him delaying it unnecessarily.

I brace myself on the back of a chair not to topple over. "I was chosen."

Mum clicks her tongue. "You silly, silly boy. You didn't want this. I didn't want it for you."

I expected her to remind me how much of an honor this is, so I'm taken aback by her response. I stand there with my jaw slack and my heart in fucking smithereens.

A sob bubbles out of her throat. "I love you, λεβέντη μου." She stands and envelops me in a hug, the both of us sobbing silently for a minute before she draws back to look into my eyes and rubs off the tears from my face with her bruised hands. "You'll be alright. You're strong and clever, so you'll do well at court. Soon enough, you'll be running the whole place, you'll see."

I open my mouth to tell her I'd rather not survive the night, but no sound comes out.

"Wise words," Jorge breathes, joining us in the kitchen. He hands me a thick binder and wraps an arm around Mum. "Miss Andreas is with her parents, now, and they'll make sure she calms down before she's arrested for treason. I'll be waiting for you in the courtyard at six, and the princess will meet you for the ceremony at sunset. Read this in the meantime."

"What is it?" Mum asks.

Jorge squeezes her shoulder. "Instructions."

She glares at the papers. "To do what?"

A gruesome table of contents outlines the main sections of the binder, and I skim the first few pages. "It's a roadmap to survive the night."

Duties of a first-blood. Court decorum. Anatomy of human veins and arteries. Without meaning to, I punch a hole in the wall. In a few hours, I'll be a slave to a demon I abhor. A part of me wishes for a swift release.

Maybe it wouldn't be so bad if I didn't survive the night.

Mum sighs as though she read my thoughts. "Leave us, Jorge. I need to speak with my son in private. Don't worry, he'll report to you on time. Callas' don't run from duty." She turns her sun-battered face to the sea. "Even when they should."

CHAPTER 4

FIRST-BLOOD

ARIELLE

The orange sphere burns over the deep blue sea, and red and pink hues fan across the glassy surface of the water. My black, freshly-painted nails click on the rails of the balcony as I breathe in the salty air.

It's my last sundown as a human. Energy surges and expands along my spine. Before the night is over, I'll be stronger, faster, and more resilient to pain.

All my life, I've been stuck in a waiting room. After my mother died, the Elders took over my education. I was told how to speak, how to act, and how to dress. I didn't belong anywhere. I couldn't form friendships with humans my age and was held apart from most of the other bloodlings because of my rank. I was told to *just wait,* all in the hope that after my Nightfall, I'd stop being just potential and become more than an obedient bloodling. I can't count the times I've been told: "When you're older." "When you're older, you'll understand." "When you're older, I'll answer your questions."

When you're older, your opinion will matter...

Tonight, I'll finally become what I was always meant to be.

"The transformation has already started." Genevieve sticks one last pin in my hair. "They say that, as a vampire, you'll be able to hear the ants scavenging for food in the gardens and count the craters on the moon."

Elbows bent, I lean on the white banister. "I expect a lot of that is flowery language. I've seen my brothers look at the moon, and their eyes are certainly not telescopes. Our race is slow to change and slower to update the reference books."

Genevieve chuckles. "There is a lot of poetic nonsense to work through in the old texts."

In the last two centuries, humanity has leaped into a new age. Technology revolutionized the world, and we adapted along with it, but in many aspects, we're still living in feudal medieval times. Knights and horses still garnish our court. Corsets and capes embellish our bodies. Not always, but often enough that it feels like my world is stuck in the past.

The sun finally drops below the horizon, and I stretch my arms above my head, trying to reign in the jitters.

Genevieve adjusts the train of my dress. The glorious design is my own, and I feel like an edgy, fairytale princess. The traditional red velvet and puffy sleeves can remain in the attic's dusty chests. I don't want to start my new life dressed as an old, stuffy maiden.

The off-shoulder neckline dips between my breasts, and black silk covers them all the way down to my stomach where the top meets the long, luscious chiffon skirt. The stitching in the silk is made to resemble black feathers because I'm an ugly duckling about to hatch. It's the first time I'm allowed to wear such a revealing gown.

Tonight, I stop being a bloodling.

Footsteps glide across the stone hall, and I look over my shoulder. Lucas slows down as he draws near, and Genevieve retreats to the hallway.

My best friend's throat bobs, and his gaze roams over me and lingers on the black fabric licking my breasts. "You look..."

My chest warms.

Lucas stares deep into my eyes like he's committing them to memory. "When you emerge, you'll be different."

I lift my chin. "I'll still be me."

He grazes one of the silver ribbons entangled in my crown of braids. "I'll miss those blue eyes."

"I might keep them."

"So few of us do." He pauses, and his gaze dips to my lips. "There's something I've got to do, Ari, and I need to do it now because I won't ever get the chance again."

I suck in a heavy breath, and my breasts stretch the fabric of my dress. Despite his vague words, there's no doubt he means to kiss me.

I angle my face to him, so ready to finally cross that line. "Alright."

A sweet burst of heat expands my chest as Lucas presses his lips to mine, and his familiar, minty scent is multiplied tenfold. He grazes my bottom lip with his teeth, cups the side of my face, and angles me for a deeper taste. I open my mouth, and his tongue greets mine, the feeling peculiar and wet, but incredibly thrilling.

I roll the silky hem of his collar between my thumb and index fingers as I pull him closer.

He presses his forehead to mine before pulling away. "I've been dreaming about this kiss for years."

The revelation sparks a fire in my belly. "Why not kiss me earlier if you've always wanted to?"

"A dream is only meant to last one night."

"All we have is one minute."

A sad smile glazes his lips. "Then I shall use it well."

It's our first, second, and last kiss. Not my very first kiss, but from now on, I'll pretend that it was.

Tomorrow, everything will be different. If we were ever to kiss again, Lucas' lips wouldn't feel cooler or fresher than mine, and the strength of his steel grip on my waist would only mirror my own. The warmth and softness of this pre-Nightfall kiss won't be reproduced, ever, and so I enjoy every second, every graze, and every breath.

I curl my fingers over his chest. "Lucas...will you still play for me? Read me poetry? Or is everything going to change?"

Lucas has royal blood, too. He was raised alongside the Delacroix bloodlings while his family raised one of my cousins. The custom shows the deep amity between our kingdoms. But, as the youngest son of king Pereira's brother, he can't ever court me, and we've both known this since before we knew anything else about marriage.

"That's up to you, Ari."

Genevieve clears her throat loudly, and Lucas sidesteps just in time for the Elder to wave me inside. Over the threshold, I throw Lucas one last glance before the heavy door shuts on my old life forever.

The ceremonial hall has been spruced up for the occasion. It's arranged like a church with a central aisle and benches on each side, but it's small. Intimate. Garlands of flowers and lights hang from the chandeliers, and roses perfume the air, their subtle floral aromas mixing with the strong smell of incense. The Delacroix sigil—a gold cross and silver rose—is carved into the stone behind the Elder.

The train of my dress scratches the plush burgundy carpet as Genevieve leads me up the aisle. Mother should be the one to do this, and my throat shrinks. I hope she'd be proud of me...

The Bringer looks a little pale in the first row, his earlier enthusiasm for the ceremony apparently gone. He looks so glum, in fact, that I struggle to keep my cool, but I know better than to ruin the sanctity of the proceedings by speaking out of turn.

My second cousin, Jason, sits on the other side of the aisle with his wife, Emilia. They are both responsible for the upkeep of the island and have been my hosts for the last four years. They are the most laid-back, effable members of my family, and though they were always nice, we never really connected.

My chosen waits by the altar, nude cotton pants hanging loosely from his rugged frame. The stark contrast between our attires is meant to signify the difference in class and power, the shedding of his will to obey mine, but I wish he'd been allowed to wear a suit. His tattoo runs from the top of his collarbone to the edge of his abdomen and depicts the inner workings of a pocket watch—the sight of his bare chest is mightily distracting.

Genevieve squeezes my hands and hurries off to sit with the Bringer.

I stand up as straight as my tall heels allow and try to meet Leopold's gaze, but the impassive, imposing human stares obstinately at the carpet.

The Elder raises his hands to the sky. "This gloried night marks the passage of our beloved princess, our dark rose, Arielle Beatrice Delacroix, into her new life. The sun sets on her as a bloodling, the moon ready to greet her into eternity."

Flowery language again. Vampires aren't immortal, but since we age the equivalent of a human year in two or three decades, I guess we're damn close.

Leopold keeps his hands clasped over his stomach and frowns at the ground.

The Elder's speech blurs in my heated ears, and I step closer to my chosen. The sinews and ridges of Leopold's muscled chest betray a thin sheen of sweat, but the room is pretty cool, so he's nervous. He's built like Thor from those human movies Lucas loves so much, and his ashy blond hair sticks out in all directions. He'll most likely cut them shorter once we're at court, but the wildness suits him.

"Now, the first-blood and his patron will pronounce their vows."

Leopold stands rigid as he recites the ancient vow. "I, Leo Callas, vow to serve and obey you, princess Arielle Beatrice Delacroix."

Leo sounds more like him than old, stuffy Leopold, and I smile.

A deep breath blows out of his tight mouth. "From this day forth until my last day, I offer you my blood, my life, and my soul of my own free will." His thick brows are stuck in a perfect line, and his voice cracks as though the words are painful on his tongue.

My heart hammers. Did he not want this? I open my mouth to ask, but a stern glare from the Elder gives me pause.

I clear my throat. "I, princess Arielle Beatrice Delacroix, accept your fealty, Leo Callas. I shall not ask of you more than you can give, and you will need of nothing. Your blood, your life, and your soul are mine to protect. Forever."

The Elder hands me the end of a thick, black rope. I grip it tightly, and he walks in circles around us, slowly tying us together. The large skirt of my dress makes it impractical for me to step forward, but soon, the space between Leo and I is reduced to an inch of crushed chiffon. The friction scatters static electricity over my thighs and causes me to shiver.

Leo rests his large hands on my waist, and I lean into his embrace. Then, like he's just now realizing what he's done, blood drains from his face, and he snaps his arms back to his sides.

My brows furrow.

Doesn't he know he's allowed to touch me? He's the only human allowed to do so without quarrels. It's almost funny how this mountain of a man is now at my mercy. It's thrilling and scary all at once.

He's so tall that I have to recline my head to look at him. The leftover stubble he had back at the choosing ceremony is gone, his jaw as smooth as the rose petals in the garden. Cologne lingers in the air, and I wonder if they forced him to shave. I don't really care for the traditional buzz cut, and I wouldn't mind if he chose to grow a beard.

After seven rotations, the Elder hands Leo the other end of the rope.

"By the dark Gods and our queen Nyx, mistress of night, I welcome you into her chambers." The Elder pushes open the thick stone door behind the altar and passes a small leather bag to Leo. "The Nightfall has begun."

CHAPTER 5

NIGHTFALL

ARIELLE

We free ourselves from the bind, the slow, polite claps of our witnesses the only sound audible as I inch inside the stone chamber with Leo on my heels. The door closes behind us, and the loud *thump* of the lock brings a chill to my bones. I swallow hard, my mouth drier than the champagne they served at brunch this morning. There's no other way out and no windows. A ripple of energy reverberates off the walls as I take in my surroundings.

This is where I'll be tested.

The white chair tucked in the corner clashes with the stone walls and the bulky, four-poster bed that towers in the center of the room. The Nightfall chamber was built over Nyx's tomb and allows the vampires who go through their Nightfall here to be reborn as the most powerful of their kin. This is why my family asserted control over the island, so we can tap into the dark power that dates back millenia.

Are the legends true, or is it like the psalms? It might just be a tradition meant to scare off our enemies.

Leo dumps the bag the Elder handed him to the ground, his

sudden movement jolting me back to reality. The infuriating man doesn't meet my gaze, and I paw at the front of my dress, unsure of what comes next.

Did I make a mistake, choosing him? He still won't look at me...

"I was born here, you know?" I tell him, trying to break the tension as I walk deeper into the room and sit on the bed. "My mother insisted on giving birth to all her children here. 'Births, weddings, and funerals must be celebrated under Nyx's eyes,' she used to say. She thought it'd give her sons enough strength to kill their enemies and her daughters beautiful crowns to rule over them."

Leo stands stock-still at the foot of the bed, his knuckles white.

I caress the ivory duvet, thinking about the countless generations of Delacroix who saw their life forever changed in this very room. "I need to tell you... I don't mind if you don't cut your hair like the others. It's an old tradition, but I like your hair as it is. And I don't care about a beard, either."

The small talk is meant to reassure him that I have no intention of killing him tonight, but still, he doesn't look at me. His throat bobs, and he doesn't say anything. Why isn't he saying anything? I pace the room back and forth, trying to think of something clever to say, acting aloof like this isn't the biggest night of my life.

The quasi-continuous tingling at the back of my throat that I've endured the last few days suddenly morphs into something else. Frost scatters across my ribs, tickles my belly button, and radiates all the way to my fingers.

Leo's breaths grow uneven as I walk toward him.

They said in the books that I should ask for his last wishes, but it's so bizarre to discuss this. Should I acknowledge the tiny possibility that I might kill him? Or are some things better left unsaid?

I rap my fingers on one of the bedposts. "If you were to die—"

"I've already said my goodbyes," he chucks out.

Short and to the point, and yet I find myself appalled by his answer. "Don't be afraid, very few first-bloods die."

"I'm not afraid."

I grip my chiffon skirt with both hands and sit on the edge of the mattress. "Then why won't you look at me?"

The starkness in Leo's green eyes is like a punch in the gut, and cold sweat drips down my back, my empty stomach clenched and painful. The hunger is here.

Blood rushes along my chosen's arteries, and his blue veins gleam, right beneath the skin. I want to touch him. Feel him. Bite him.

"I'm so hungry for you, Leo," I whimper, the weight of the moment catching up to me all at once. I glide closer and rest one palm over his furious heart. "What if I can't stop?"

He shrugs away the possibility. "I'll die."

My hand shakes over his solid chest. "How can you say it like it's no big deal?"

"Is it?"

"I don't want to kill you, Leo." I wet my lips, my gaze riveted on his neck.

A long shiver passes through him. "You shouldn't start at the neck, then."

The suggestion gives me pause. "What?"

"You should bite my wrist first. It'll be easier to deal with if you... make a mess."

My mouth fills with saliva as I flip his large hand over and trace the deep lines in his palm, the rough calluses of his hands scattering goosebumps over my neck. "I won't be able to make it feel good. Not yet. There's an art to the bite. Time, power, and control will allow me to make it pleasurable to mortals—to you."

Leo shakes his head forcefully. "That's fine."

"It'll hurt," I explain more clearly, thinking he doesn't understand. The gossip in town probably never mentioned how painful the bite can be. After all, the normals there gladly volunteer to feed our family's envoys in exchange for the heady pleasure it procures.

"I prefer it if it hurts."

Is he a pain junkie? Is that why he volunteered? Despite the throng of questions spiraling in my brain, my teeth chatter, and I graze his pulse point with my fingertips. Fangs pierce my inflamed gums for the first time. A wince escapes me at the sharp, foreign sensation, but I run my tongue over them, curious.

"Hurry up," Leo growls.

My jaw ticks. How dare he rush me in this moment?

The hollow thuds of his quickened pulse drown out my admonishment. My nostrils flare, alive with wildly different aromas than the ones I'm used to. Leo's dry, masculine scent lulls me closer. Sand and salt mix with fear over his thick, smooth wrist. Fumes of despair tickle the back of my throat, and a bottomless hunger rattles my chest.

My brand new set of teeth nicks his offered flesh, and velvety blood coats my tongue, hot and rich. The luxurious taste of salt, musk, and citrus drives me wild, and I tear through his soft flesh without mercy, widening the small puncture wound to a large gash. Leo grasps a fist of my hair, tearing me away from his wrist with a strong grip, his precious blood trickling to the ground. A hiss escapes me, my transformation incomplete, but instead of warding me off, he wrenches me up to his neck. The sight of his jugular cramps my stomach with need as my heart swells to the size of a sun and beats long and hard in my chest.

One. Last. Beat.

Teeth pierce flesh. Blood flows.

Ecstasy crashes into my veins as his life essence flows into me, binding us in a macabre dance of dominance and submission.

Tingles and needles scatter across my neck, my breasts, my arms and legs... Nightfall comes in powerful, unforgiving waves like a million ants marching in to wage war against my mortal flesh. Cell by cell, it tears me down and molds me into something else. Something better, darker, and a tiny bit evil.

Thunder rumbles across my muscles as Leo spices up my mouth, throat, and belly. It's a craving I've never known. The cold is gone, replaced by Leo's heat. Borrowed heat. Stolen life. I want to bathe in Leo's blood.

I shove him down on the bed and swallow gulp after gulp, each of them more delicious and empowering than the last.

Hunger turns to greed. Girl becomes demon.

One delicious pulse after another, blood sprays the roof of my mouth. My prey's heart tumbles once. Twice.

I blink, my eyes open to the room I'm laying in, to the clothes I designed, to the man I chose to drink.

Prey? No. Leo. A man. My first-blood.

With a whimper, I tear myself away. He lays on the bed, white as the satin sheets beneath him. My hand flies to my blood-stained lips.

He's too pale, and his heartbeats are sluggish.

I killed him.

Panic swells in my chest, and I tear a piece of linen and tie a tourniquet above his wrist. The river of red stops flowing, but his mangled neck still gapes open, so I press a bunched sheet to the hole, but blood gorges the satin, mocking me.

My gaze darts to the stony doorway. It's useless to knock or shout because they won't interfere. The door will not open until morning, and by then, Leo will be dead.

What am I missing?

Chiffon chafes my thighs as I jump off the bed and rummage through the bag Leo brought with him. The binder at the bottom catches my attention, and my eyes skitter across the pages. It's a how-to guide for the night.

If the vampire lets you drink from him first, you'll have better chances at survival.

Leo kept this from me on purpose. Why? I scurry over to him and bite my arm. A grimace twists my face at the horrid taste of my own blood—cold and dull and metallic.

The red liquid trickles down to Leo's full lips, and the sight almost sends me over the edge. My beast desperately wants things to go the other way around.

The ecstasy brought on by my first-blood, my first taste, will know no equal. I need to safeguard it at all cost, and the thought of losing it forever tames my beast into submission.

With a grunt, I jam my wrist inside his mouth, and he finally swallows. I wait until he's gulped down at least five mouthfuls before walking away.

Holding my breath to block his scent, I tear down the skirt of my gown, cast it aside, and perch on the white velvet lounge chair in the corner, as far away from Leo as possible.

His short breaths grow steadier. Massive and yet frail, he hangs between life and death for a few hours. No matter how hard I try, I cannot look away. The windowless room grows quiet as a tomb except for the timid thuds of Leo's heart, and a languid fatigue claims me whole.

Just as I'm about to doze off, a painful clarity strikes me, and my eyes snap back open.

Leo wanted to die.

Leo stirs on the bed, and the mattress creaks under his weight, his scent luring me closer. I unfold my legs and walk to the halfway point between us to test my resolve. "Good morning."

Leo doesn't answer.

My new vampire eyes see everything better. The knots in the wood of the headrest form tight, concentric circles. Tiny cracks in the bedside table betray the age of the furniture. Dead skin flakes off Leo's thumb, and a slightly darker swell of ink highlights the edges of his tattoo.

Leo's irises are no longer *green*, but the color of freshly bloomed leaves mixed with gold speckles and a hint of seaweed. The difference is so immense that my heart gives a big squeeze—it doesn't beat as it used to, but it's not dead either.

The stone door of the chamber inches open, and my ears buzz. Servants chat in the kitchens, waves storm over the rocks, and pigeons squabble for dried raisins on the roof. Rays of sunlight filter in from the opened door and undulate across the room like golden snakes.

It's all so loud and bright and confusing.

Above all, the feel of Leo's skin lingers. They explained that I might remain sensitive to sound and lights for a few days, and that in time, I'd be able to pick and choose what to tune out, but right now, it *hurts*.

The first test of my self-control is the human doctor who comes to check on Leo. When he arrives, I rush back to the chair and cross my legs beneath me. Holding my breath, I watch as he hooks Leo up to a bag of fluids before cleaning up his wounds and bandaging them. The white gauze covers the mouth-watering gashes, making it slightly easier for me not to obsess over them.

The stranger's scent sticks to the air after his departure, tempting me to run after him.

Pressure coils in my belly, but I will not let my beast dictate my faith. I am a Delacroix.

The second test is a young handmaid who comes to change Leo's bandages a few hours later. She eyes me sideways, her frazzled heartbeats unnerving as hell as she completes her job quickly and skitters out.

The last test is Genevieve.

"Congratulations, *ma chérie*."

"I almost killed him."

She glances at Leo's sleeping form. "He didn't ask to drink from you before it started, did he?"

"No."

She presses her creased lips together.

"Why does he want to die?" I ask, still at a loss. "I did nothing wrong."

"Oh, *ma chérie*, it's not about you." She sets a gold cup on the table between us and pries a dagger from her robes.

"I can't—"

"I trust you." She slices her wrist and fills the shimmering mug.

My muscles go rigid, and yet I resist the urge to leap forward and drink from her neck, my whole body shaking.

This is the last part of the ritual.

"Thank you for your loyalty, Genevieve Damora. You have served us well," I whisper, knowing I'll never see her again.

"Your mother would be so proud of you."

My eyes sting. "I wish she was here..."

Her hand immobilizes in mid-air, as though she just remembered she can no longer touch me. "Don't bow down to injustice, and always fight for what you believe in."

"Goodbye, Genevieve. May the dark Gods smile upon you."

"And you, my Arielle. *Ma petite sirène.*"

I clasp my jade pendant as she walks away.

She's the last person alive who knew my mother like I did, and now she'll vanish from my life forever, her services to the crown fulfilled now that I've transitioned. The golden cup she left behind beckons, so I snatch it off the table, tilt my head back, and gulp it down until there's nothing left.

CHAPTER 6
ANYTHING
LEO

The hospital wing beneath the Delacroix's estate is well-equipped to transfuse and rehydrate a servant. It comes with the territory, I guess. It hasn't been 24 hours since the princess almost drained me dry, and I'm bitter that she didn't finish the job.

The discarded hospital gown forms a blue clump at my feet as I change, ready to meet the obligations of my non-life. I hate how smooth and sharp my muscles feel, a sure proof that her cursed blood healed me quicker and more thoroughly than the doctors did. Most of all, I loathe that I almost died with her blood in my system, which would have turned me into one of them.

Humans turned vampires aren't as powerful or sturdy as the natural-born vampires, but they certainly feed as much as their counterparts do. I'd rather die than become a watered-down, feeble version of the bloodsuckers that rule this world.

A man enters my room just as I'm done pulling my jeans up.

"Don't you knock?" I snap, adjusting my belt in a hurry. The rules might be different here, but knocking before invading someone's room is Human 101.

He holds his palms in front of him. "Fuck. Sorry."

I shrug and wrangle my white t-shirt over my head.

"I'm Quentin, Lord Pereira's first-blood." The newcomer extends his hand. He's got short hair, and he's young. Younger than me.

His goofy smile rings a bell.

"You're Trent's brother, right? I went to school with him. I didn't know you'd been chosen." I didn't keep up with the island's gossip after I left for the continent, but Trent was a good friend of mine in high school, so I shake his intrusive brother's hand.

"Yes. My parents were stoked. Come, Jean wants to speak with you." He motions me forward.

"Now? The doctor just gave me the green light to get up from that wretched bed."

"Yes, mate. Welcome to the rest of your life. We're always on the clock." Quentin guides me to the back of the big house, where the servants live.

The sun is hidden behind the clouds, and the alluring smell of bread and yeast sparks gurgles in my belly. In the interior courtyard, we cross paths with a trio of women carrying groceries, and they stare at me like I'm a fucking movie star.

I hide my hands in my pockets and drag my feet along the paved stones. "Why are they staring?"

"You almost didn't make it, mate. She almost killed you. That would have been—" he mimes an explosion at his temples.

The queasiness in my belly doubles, and I swallow a ball of saliva. "Vampires kill people all the time."

"Not on this island, and certainly not their first-blood."

"She'll have another go at it soon enough. Keeping my fingers crossed."

A chuckle escapes him. "You're funny."

We emerge into an office tucked at the bottom of the exterior staircase where Jorge called out my name after brunch, and sweat gathers on my forehead. What am I doing here? I should be dead.

"Leo, this is Jean, first-blood to Jason Delacroix," Quentin says.

A desk stands between us, but the frail man doesn't extend his hand. Instead, he glares at me above the round, tiny glasses that rest on the tip of his aquiline nose.

After a few long seconds, Jean motions for me to sit, but I shake my head.

"I have to go over the rules of the household with you." He opens the highest cupboard behind his desk. "You will present yourself to the princess every day at sunset, and any other time she wishes. You'll take care of her day-to-day needs, and oversee her staff. The details of the schedule and an all-around summary of your duties are in your new phone." He passes me a sleek black smartphone. "Quentin will show you the kitchens."

I glide the phone into my pocket, baffled by their nonchalant behavior. "Anything else?"

Quentin and Jean act as though they're training me for a new job and showing me the ropes. They don't look somber at all, and maybe it's a good sign, but I mostly think they've been brainwashed.

Jean plucks a bottle from the shelf, along with a wide, oval-shaped tube. "You will eat well, drink at most one glass of wine a day, and exercise four times a week so your blood, body, and mind remain strong and fresh." The bottle rattles, full of pills, as he hands it over. "You'll take these supplements once a day before going to bed."

"What are they?" I eye the pills suspiciously. Is everyone here drugged? Is that why they're so docile?

"Iron, vitamins, a magical booster to regenerate your red blood cells, and something to help your circadian cycle adjust to living at night. Take them, or one of these days you'll faint, and they'll give you injections instead." He passes along the tube, too. "The ointment is for your wounds. Apply a thin coat on each bite mark, and they'll heal in mere hours. Royals prefer a flawless skin."

Dread and a hint of mind-numbing sarcasm builds in my chest. "Why shouldn't they want their meat fresh?"

Quentin heads for the door, but not before I see him shiver. "I have stuff to do. Meet me in the kitchens when you're done."

Jean closes the door to his office behind Quentin as he leaves. "Watch your attitude, boy. If you don't, your family will suffer the consequences."

The threat slaps me back to reality, and I give Jean a grave nod.

He snatches a white, old-fashioned tissue from his front pocket and cleans his glasses. "You'll be fed by the same staff as the princess. Please inform them of any allergies for tonight's dinner, but don't get too comfortable. The princess leaves for court tomorrow. Things work pretty much the same at the castle, except for the amount of decorum. Things are relaxed here. At court, you'll have to know how to address the lords and ladies correctly. You might even cross the dark king's path."

"Alright."

He rests both hands on the desk. "There are a few books you should read. I'll make a list. What you do from seven in the morning to sundown is your business. Get enough sleep, though. You may engage in sexual intercourse with any willing *human*."

I raise my hands in alarm. "That won't be necessary."

The old man's eyes soften. "Believe me, boy. A lifetime of abstinence isn't as honorable as it sounds. As the princess' first-blood, and given your looks, you'll be somewhat of a catch. Nyx's children are completely off-limits. And don't make the mistake of falling in love. You must follow the princess wherever she goes, and you can't afford to form attachments. The blue pills in the bottle will ensure that you can't accidentally father an offspring—"

"Condoms don't cut it for vampires?"

He observes me with a frosty pout. "If a woman became pregnant with your child, she'd be executed."

I rub my face down. "Shit—okay, I got it."

Abstinence or blue pills. Fuck.

"Good." Jean opens the top drawer of his desk and retrieves a velvet bag. He unfastens the threads and flashes me a signet ring.

"This is the princess' personal mark. There's a slight darker tint to the rose, you see? It will warn other children of the night of who you are. If any of them were to bite you anyway, they'd be in big trouble."

I barely glance at the mark. "Just call them vampires, please."

Jean clicks his tongue. "Fine. No other vampire shall taste you. I'll tattoo the mark at the base of your right ear. Moisturize it a few times a day, and avoid unnecessary exposure to sunlight." He powers on a wireless tattoo pen.

I swallow hard. "I've got other tattoos. I know how it works."

"Sit down then, so I can get to work."

I finally sit, drained by this insane conversation. The pen buzzes to life, and the needle stings more as it pierces my skin than it usually does. I don't want this tattoo. This brand—because that's what it is—makes me sick. We're nothing but livestock to them.

"The only vampire who is allowed to touch you is the princess. You belong to her. Never forget that," Jean breathes, his fingers soft on the shell of my ear.

"I won't," I ground out.

The needle pierces my skin again and again. I grip the armrests not to punch Jean in the face.

"If she asks for anything, you shall provide it," he adds.

"Yes."

The old man pauses. "*Anything.*"

I grit my teeth, his heavy-handed allusion to sex perfectly clear. I can't believe my life has come to this. I'm a common whore.

He sets the tattoo pen aside and rubs his chin, apparently lost in thought. "There will come a time in the next year when the princess will enter a fertile period. You'll have to know the signs so you can take the right precautions..."

Great. A crash course in the female vampire menstrual cycle is what I need right now.

After he's done briefing me about the female anatomy and the merits of contraception, I join Quentin in the kitchens. The big room allows for many cooks to work together, with sinks, stoves, stainless steel appliances, and a big island in the middle.

The man offers me a beer, and I snap off the cork and chug down half of it in one gulp.

Quentin raises his own bottle in cheer. "Don't look so glum, mate. We're leaving for France soon, that'll be fun."

"You're looking forward to this?"

"Absolutely. Victor Delacroix is the mighty king of Europe. To demons, he's the only force of law. Vampires have helmed the supernatural world for two millennia, and the Delacroix night court is the most powerful kingdom of all. We're going to see stuff most people never even hear about."

The admiration in his voice turns my stomach.

"Delightful." I blast past the delivery door and sit on the top of the stone staircase outside. The sun hangs low in the sky, falling quickly under the edge of the sea, and my skin tingles because of what it means.

The next vampire bite is coming for me, and fast.

Quentin sits beside me. "Are you so blue because of that blonde bombshell? My brother always said you were the luckiest son of a bitch alive. What was her name? Zara?"

I grunt in response, the beer heavy in my hand.

"Your old flame doesn't hold a candle to the princess, in my humble opinion. You lucky bastard. You might actually get to tap that." He tilts his back to the sky with his eyes half-mast. "I've seen her on the beach in her bikini." He smacks his lips together.

A cynical smile escapes me. "Are you having lots of sex with your vampire?" I'm getting serious *bro* vibes from this guy, and bros don't like to think about anal sex unless a woman is the one on the receiving end.

Quentin spits out a mouthful of beer. "God, no. Lucas is fresh and green as a baby fern."

We drink in silence for a moment, looking at the sunset.

"Chin up, Callas. You never know. Genevieve Damora survived the princess' mother, so you might get lucky."

I freeze at his answer. "Are you implying the princess might die before I do?"

He shrugs in response. "If you're brooding for freedom, it's the only hope you've got."

"It's treason," I enunciate loudly.

Is he testing me? I wouldn't put it past Jean to test my allegiance through Quentin.

My *colleague* flashes a quick smirk. "Come on, mate. It's just us here. And I'm not the one who looks destroyed by his new title—you are."

"Have you heard something?"

He rubs the back of his neck. "I was just saying we never know what might happen. Don't read into it." His gaze dips to the ground at the last second, and he stands to leave. "I just wanted to cheer you up."

My chest cramps. I can't shake this feeling...as though Quentin knows more than he lets on. He clearly regrets mentioning it, so Jean didn't put him up to it.

Electricity buzzes in my palms and sweat pearls on my forehead. My instincts scream at me that something is amiss, and that the princess is in real danger.

CHAPTER 7
LUCKY
ARIELLE

Who said darkness was black? The night has never held so much fascination. So many colors.

Midnight-blue waves roll over their velvety undertow in hues so deep and crisp that my eyes water. A splendid moon with yellow craters winks overhead, and the sky shimmers with purple and burgundy strokes. Roses perfume the air with aromas so thick and rich that I want to drag each of their luscious, satin petals across my tongue.

Jason and Emilia smile at me like a pair of hens watching their ducklings test the feel of a pond for the first time.

"How are you adjusting? Well, I think," Jason asks politely.

"Yes."

The evening has been a blur of colors, smells, and sounds. I waited for the sun to set before joining them on the balcony, its direct rays still too dangerous for my newborn skin.

I feel... awake. Alive. Energized.

Like my old life was merely a dream—or rather a slumber.

A full golden cup warms my hands, and I raise it to my lips, enthralled by the spicy taste of Leo's blood. I drank too much from him last night, and I didn't want to risk another slip, so when he came to me at sundown, I asked him to use a butterfly needle and tube to serve me a cup of his blood.

The powder that prevents the blood from clotting tastes weird. Maybe it's primitive, but I can't wait for my control to improve and his wounds to heal so I can sink my teeth into him again. I stare down at my hands, eager to experiment how different textures feel with this new skin. How Leo feels—

A loud ring blares into my sensitive eardrums, and my hand flies to cover my ears at the intensity of the sound.

Jason snaps his old-fashioned cell phone open. "Yes, the princess is here with me." A big frown twists his face. "No, why?"

I'm supposed to leave for court tomorrow, so I'm looking forward to a quiet, uneventful night. I haven't seen Lucas, yet, and I can't wait to see him with my enhanced-but-still-totally-blue eyes. I'm so glad I got to keep them, the shade so similar to my mother's— almost bluer than the old ones.

After a long pause, listening to whoever is on the other side of the conversation, Jason adds, "Is that really necessary?"

Emilia places her small hand on her husband's shoulder. "Is everything okay?"

Jason's red gaze darts to me as he hangs up. "Yes, but they sent a royal guard."

"A royal guard?" I ask. "Why?"

"They want him to escort you back to France."

A shiver shakes through me at the somber tone of his voice. Royal guards exist outside of our army's normal command structure, and most of them are better skilled at violence than protection.

Jason peers over the railing to the tortuous path leading to the house. "Look. He's already here."

In the distance, a tall silhouette stalks from the fog, each step confident and soundless. The soldier walks exactly as my father's guards used to—with deadly intent. A nervous shiver slices through me, and I rub my arms. Long-forgotten memories rise to the surface.

A guard plucks me from my bed and throws me over his shoulders. A scream tears from my throat, and I ram my small fists against his large, gargantuan back, but he drags me to a cold and dark closet and crushes his palm to my mouth until I taste blood on my tongue. The thick red carpet lining the closet chafes my knees.

A cold patch prickles my neck. The man didn't hurt me. In fact, he was just doing his job, but the aftermath was no better for it.

The guard becomes bigger and bigger until he disappears beyond the corner of the estate. Another minute passes before he marches onto the balcony with long strides. A thick pair of aviator sunglasses obscures his face, and shadows thicken around the edges of his skin like a personal devil travels behind him, his large shoulders highlighted by his fancy suit. A black undershirt hugs his torso, and the red lines on the turn-down collar mark him as a high-ranking member of the royal guard.

He bows his head as he draws near, greeting me according to my rank. "Alec Beaumont, at your service, your royal highness."

The moonlight finally reaches his face and licks the sharp angle of his jaw, a discreet earpiece tucked in his right ear.

My eyes narrow at the mention of his surname. "Is my brother well?" I coat my words up in thick ice so my fear doesn't pierce through.

The Beaumont brothers have got a terrible reputation, and of the three of them, Alec is the most...infamous. Strong and deadly on the battlefield, but arrogant and impetuous at court. Why would Victor send his best *assassin* to protect me?

Alec Beaumont braces his hands at his front, a gun tucked in a holster at his right hip. "Yes. The king is eager to see you and asked me to escort you back to the castle."

"Why is a royal guard needed for a simple plane ride?" I ask.

"I obey orders, princess. I do not pretend to understand them." The sharp edge in his voice is a direct jab at my brother's choice. Clearly, he's as displeased by the situation as I am.

Jason cuts in. "Watch your tone, Beaumont."

44

The difference between the two vampires is glaring. Royals are usually thin, and Jason is no exception, whereas Alec Beaumont is all length and muscles.

I turn to my cousin. "Is there a specific threat? Am I in danger?"

Jason slides back a few feet, putting more distance between him and Alec. "I don't know, your highness."

My blood races at my temples. He's lying. We might not have become friends during my stay, but I've never seen him so jumpy.

"You're hiding something from me, I can tell. Tell me what you know," I order.

Jason rubs his hand over his beard, taken aback by my guile, but I'm a full-fledged vampire now, and I do outrank him.

"With Ludovic's death, the Zhaos have been sniffing around the island..." he trails off.

"Why wasn't I informed?"

"The king and prime minister thought better not to trouble you with politics."

The sexist bastards. I knew they'd pull this kind of nonsense.

Beaumont clears his throat. He stood so still and silent while Jason and I were arguing that I had almost forgotten he was there. Vampires are attuned to movements, making it easy for us to track our prey... The royal guard clearly knows how to use that to his advantage.

"I have orders from the king. We shall leave immediately," he says.

"I haven't packed—"

"Your staff can pack your things. Take only what is necessary for the voyage, and we'll leave at once."

"Is that wise?" Jasons asks.

"The king gave me strict instructions."

Jason holds both palms up in front of him. "Of course, of course. I'll have my staff ready the plane at once."

My blood boils. How dare he speak to us the way you speak to rowdy children? "I really do not care for your tone, Mr. Beaumont."

He might have a hundred years on me, but he looks barely thirty, so it's not like he's an Elder or anything. In fact, anyone less than two-hundred years old is basically still a teenager in our world.

"Excuse me, your *royal highness*. I'm a soldier, not a gentleman." The fake honey in his apology is as stiff and dishonest as his curt bow.

I turn around in anger, making a mental note to tell the king about the guard's unacceptable behavior, and head to my room.

I've just finished changing into a short black skirt and a white blouse when a soft knock on the door interrupts my outraged train of thoughts. I close my eyes and breathe in deep, the familiar thuds of Leo's heartbeat calling out to me from the other side of the wood.

"Come in, Leo."

He enters the room with his arms braced at his sides, fists curled. "I've been informed of our hasty departure, princess. Do you wish to feed before we travel?"

My heart softens, his fear as easy to see as the leftover bite marks on his neck. "That won't be necessary. Just ask Selene to get me my favorite bag, the one with the gold and silver sequins."

"As you wish." He doubles back to find Selene with a slight bow, his fist uncurling.

All the other humans were only temporarily assigned to me, so he's the only one that'll come along. There's no time to say goodbye to my handmaidens, no time to do this right. I grab my mother's ring, my letter sealer, and the family tree my father drew by hand.

My diary is tucked between ribbons and necklaces, and I pry it from the bedside table. As I flip the pages, my elegant script runs along the paper, and my throat tightens. This journal contains the essence of my soul. I've been writing in it for years, consigning my thoughts and feelings in ink.

My hand shakes a little as I stride forward and throw it into the fireplace. A puff of ash and glittering embers rise into the air, but I turn my back on the book's already blackened corners.

I'm not a kid anymore. I can't afford to have my personal musings found by the wrong people.

Leo returns and hands me the requested bag with Emilia on his heels, the long skirt of her dress flowing in the breeze. "I'm sorry you have to rush out. Let us deal with your belongings. We'll send them after you in a few hours with your first-blood."

I swallow hard, my mouth dry. "We won't travel together?"

Emilia fails to mask a wince, her dislike for Alec Beaumont plain as day. "The royal guard insisted, but I'm sure you'll be reunited before dawn so you can feed."

Leo nods, his head bent in submission. I throw the leather strap of my duffel bag over my shoulder and stroll through my room one last time. I'm thankful for the change, really. Besides Lucas, the life I built here was empty, and I hope my undead life will not follow the same pattern.

A black armored car is waiting for me at the foot of the estate, and Emilia hugs me awkwardly. "Safest travels, princess."

The fabric of her blue dress glides along my arms, fresh and smooth, as I give her a quick hug. "Thank you for your hospitality."

Jason nods in acknowledgment, and I turn to my impolite bodyguard.

Beaumont stands in front of the black Range Rover, hands braced together at his front, gazing dead ahead like we're invisible to him and he to us—the perfect picture of professionalism.

He opens the door for me as I draw near and makes sure to close the door behind me before walking around the car to the driver seat. The short trip to the edge of the property where the landing strip is located is quick and silent, and we board the small private plane waiting for us there in silence.

I haven't been on a plane in years, and a tingle of excitement shivers through me. The interior of the aircraft is spotless. Three rows of seats stand on each side of the aisle, each of them located next to a large porthole, and a sleek white quartz bar with a matching couch form a living room area in the back.

I freeze, one hand gripping the headrest of the closest seat. "Where is Lucas? He was supposed to travel with me."

Alec ignores my questions and exchanges a few words with the flight attendant.

A black and white uniform hugs the blond woman's curves, a few buttons of her blouse undone to emphasize her cleavage. She's human, about my age, and the scent of her blood dries up my mouth.

"Mr. Beaumont," I snap, commanding my escort's attention.

My curt question wipes the dashing smile from his face. "Lord Pereira is taking a different plane."

"Who decided that?"

"Me."

"On whose authority?"

"Mine."

"How dare you—"

The corners of his mouth quirk. "Her majesty might outrank me at dinner parties, but I've been tasked with your well-being. Any matter of security falls on me and me alone, and no amount of whining will change that. As long as the threat remains unclear, we shall be quick and discreet."

My mouth opens and closes in outrage, my fists balled at my sides. "If discretion is so important, why did you allow a random human to tag along?"

He removes his sunglasses and tucks them inside his jacket, the golden ring shining around his otherwise typical garnet eyes surprisingly clear. "You're a newborn vampire. It's always better to keep a snack on hand."

I sit in the front row, convinced this gorgeous woman is here for him, not me—he certainly looks eager to get a bite out of her. "Is she really here for my benefit, or yours?"

I've heard other...stories about the assassin. Scandalous tales, really.

Alec grins, and an elusive dimple adorns his cheek. "Aren't you curious to see how pleasurable the bite can be?"

48

I squirm in my seat, the words *pleasurable* and *bite* heating up my chest. "I wouldn't want *you* to teach me."

Unperturbed, the obnoxious guard presses on his ear piece. "Ready for takeoff. Lucky is secured."

I whip my head around to face him. "Lucky?"

His shoulders hitch in a careless shrug. "It's your codename."

"I don't care for it." The plane wobbles forward, and I grip the armrests of my seat.

He winks at me—fucking winks at me—like I'm a schoolgirl and he's fucking Prince Charming. *"Would her majesty prefer spoiled? Or snooty?"*

My mouth opens to call him out for being an absolute asshole when an unfamiliar, ticklish sensation warms the back of my ears, and I stagger at the realization that Beaumont didn't speak those words aloud...he merely *thought* them. Reading minds isn't a run-of-the-mill vampire trait, and my eyes bulge at the implications. Either that, or my transformation into a vampire wrecked my brain, and I'm hearing random insults.

Beaumont waves the attendant over and murmurs a few words in her ear as I gape, unable to speak.

"You look pale as a ghost, your highness," he points out with a gleeful edge to his voice.

My fangs unsheathe of their own accord. "I'll have you fired, Mr. Beaumont," I growl, my voice lower than I've ever heard it.

Alec tilts his head back and laughs, the sound so joyful and boyish that it's actually worse than a slap in the face. He sits down in the seat on the other side of the aisle and drums a happy beat on his thighs, gazing out at the runway. "You can try, Lucky. You can try."

CHAPTER 8

ASSASSIN

ALEC

Two and a half hours after take-off, I stretch my legs and walk to the bar at the back of the plane. "A beer, please."

The flight attendant nods and bends down to access the fridge tucked underneath the counter. I spin around and lean on the bar, bored.

No good deed goes unpunished. If I hadn't let Eleanore escape, I'd be managing covert ops or running security for the coronation. Instead, I'm stuck on a tiny plane babysitting a teenager. I've suffered through worse than a three hour plane ride with a royal, but I can't wait for this charade to be over.

A spoiled princess. How original.

My last-minute decision to have her friend catch a later plane was pure gold. Jesus, she was pissed. She still is, sitting in the luxurious leather seat with her arms braced tightly around her frame. The black plaid skirt and white silky blouse make her look as human as she possibly can, but power radiates off her pale skin.

Raven black hair. High cheekbones. Chin held high because she believes she's better than me...

She's a Delacroix, that's for sure.

A bit of the family's black magic clearly flows in her veins. Maybe I should be careful, or I'll end up cursed. Witches don't have the monopoly on spells, and this girl-turned-vampire could cast a fog over any man's brain.

She's tall and lean, but with more muscles and curves than her royal counterparts. The older Delacroix catered the perfect dry shape of high-born vampires for decades, while this one is still fresh and plump, her appetite for human food only just withering.

Red, heart-shaped lips contrast with her perfectly smooth alabaster skin, topped off by the most striking blue eyes. It's so unfair that she got to keep her human coloring. She didn't need something other than her name and beauty to set her apart.

"Our princess is...ethereal," the flight attendant muses under her breath.

"I guess." My brows pull together. I don't like that she caught me staring.

She walks around the bar and hands me the beer I ordered. "Her resemblance to her late mother will certainly spark a few battles for her affection."

I offer the blonde a fake smile and discourage any further discussion by returning to my seat.

A few minutes later, she comes over to retrieve the empty bottle. "Do you need *anything* else?" The floral scent of her blood tugs at my self-control as she leans closer than necessary, bending over so much that my knuckles are grazing her dangling breast.

"No," I scowl.

Christ, when did she take off her bra?

A human employee isn't supposed to act so brazenly. Not while I'm on duty. If she wants to fuck *after* the flight, fine, but something about her confidence rubs me the wrong way.

Eager for some peace, I enter the plane's cockpit and shut the door.

The pilot is part of Jason's pathetic staff, and a hint of white shows at his temples. He jerks upward with a start at my arrival. "Geez! Don't sneak up on a pilot. I didn't hear you come in."

My older brother Garrett used to call me the night owl. No vampire can move as swiftly and silently as me, but an owl isn't exactly cool. I would have preferred a lion or a tiger as a nickname, but I do see and hear better than most of my kind, and my sixth sense is tingling. A hint of warning tickles my spine as I gaze down at the old pilot.

He glances at me sideways. "Who are you, son? You're not part of my Lord's security team."

"Who I am is none of your business, and I'm not your son."

Sweat pearls over his brow. "You're from the castle?"

I click my tongue. *Fucking Jason stuck me with a moron who can't recognize a royal guard when he sees one? What the fuck.*

A runway comes into view, and all the hairs at the back of my neck stand at attention. Something's wrong. It's too soon.

"Wait. Don't land."

Rain blurs the scenery below us, but I'm almost sure we're nowhere near where we should be.

"Excuse me, sir?" The pilot coughs.

"Go back up. Now! We're not in the right place."

"I'm afraid that's not possible, sir."

The moonlight catches the end of his dagger. I block his arm in mid-air, twist it behind his back, snap his neck, and discard his body to the floor. My hands grip the "W" shaped yoke control before I can formulate a thought. I've flown plenty of planes—*fifty* years ago. There weren't so many screens and buttons then, but I stop our descent and check the navigation system.

Perpignan... what the fuck? We're miles from the estate.

My charge barrels inside the room, her voice high and squeaky. "The horny flight attendant just tried to *stake* me. What the hell is going on?"

"We were set up."

She dashes over the pilot's body and sits next to me, her mouth and chin dripping with blood. "Do you know how to fly this thing?"

"In theory." An alarm beeps loudly, and I fumble around with a few buttons to shut it up, but nothing seems to work as it should. "I think the commands have been tampered with. Grab your phone."

"I don't have one."

I grit my teeth at the ridiculousness of that. "In my pocket."

Her fingers stop shy of my leg. "I'm not groping your thigh, Mr. Beaumont."

"Give me a fucking second. I'm busy." I retrieve my cell phone and pass it to her.

"Password?"

"1897."

She snickers. "Is that the year you were born? Very secure."

I recite my little brother's number, reigning in the urge to flip her off. "Put it on speaker."

The shrill dial tone annoys me to no end, but he finally answers. "What do you want? This is a secure line—"

"Jasper, I need an extraction team for Lucky near Perpignan. ASAP."

"What the fuck are you talking about? We weren't expecting you until tomorrow."

Another high-pitch series of beeps blares from the alarm system, and I press a few buttons at random. "I changed the schedule and sent you the details."

Silence takes over the line for a second. "You certainly didn't."

"We've been set up. The pilot was bringing us directly into an ambush." I force a deep breath down my lungs. "Sending our coordinates."

The princess' manicured nails skim the screen closest to her. "You have no idea what you're doing, do you? This is the sensor control. The fuel tank is almost empty."

The sensor blinks rapidly, and I grimace. "Where should we land? We're running out of fuel."

After a long minute, Jasper finally answers, "Go north-east. There's a highway near your position that's closed for renovations. I'll have a unit meet you there in fifteen minutes."

"We'll be there." Arielle hangs up the phone with one tap and buckles down next to me. "Vampires can't be killed by plane crashes, right?"

"No, but we can be dusted by the explosion that would follow." I concentrate on the computer navigation screen and realize the princess is right. This is more of a glorified cellphone than the planes I used to fly as a rookie, and with her help, the plane finally starts heading in the right direction.

"Let's try to land this thing."

Eyes fixed on the fuel screen, she nods. "I'm with you there, Mr. Beaumont."

"How do you know so much about planes, anyway?" I ask without thinking, my tongue loosened by the wild adrenaline pumping through me.

She stares dead ahead. "My mother was a pilot."

Of course. I'm such an idiot for asking. Think, Alec, before you open your big mouth.

I bite my tongue not to say the wrong thing, knowing I'm digging my own grave here and only giving her ammunition to act on her earlier threat. The memory of our late queen is most sacred, and prying into her relationship with her daughter is stupid at best.

Black clouds overcome the sky, and I fly low until an empty strip of highway comes into view. We manage to land the plane without crashing it despite the heavy downpour. Thank our mother Nyx for that.

Four royal guard black and red SUVs barrel down the empty highway in our direction a minute later. With a deep, cleansing breath, I stand up, dust off my uniform, and adjust my cufflinks.

The princess steps over the pilot's corpse with a disgusted pout. "These people meant to kill me."

A crack of thunder rocks the air as I open the hatch. "I think they originally planned on kidnapping you. They only attacked when they realized they'd been found out."

"Why would they kidnap me?" she asks, grabbing her duffel bag from the ground.

"Because you're a princess."

She freezes in the doorway. "You say the word like it's dirty."

I unfold an umbrella and offer her my arm. "I don't know what you mean. I've devoted my life to protecting your family, your highness."

With a scoff, she barrels past me, unconcerned by the rain. "Your devotion is appreciated." She bee-lines for the closest car, and I follow in her wake, fast enough to open the door for her, but my gallantry only seems to anger her further.

Jude climbs out of the driver seat and shouts over the downpour. "You okay?"

I pass a hand over my feverish face, trying to recall all the details of the day, wondering when and where I was fooled. And by whom. Jason hired the pilot, but he's no politician, and if Jasper didn't get my messages... "Yes, but someone from our side fucked me over."

Brows furrowed in a grim line, he slaps the roof of the car. "First thing first, let's get her safely to the palace. We can figure out who screwed you after."

With a quick nod, I discard the umbrella and slip into the back with my charge. I remember how cold and overwhelming the rain felt in the beginning. How every drop resonated across my skin as it crashed, the wet sensation multiplied to the point of insanity.

She's soaking wet, and shiver after shiver quakes her body. Dark locks stick to her neck and shirt, the water making her white blouse almost transparent.

I shrug off my jacket. "Here."

She looks like the last thing she wants to do is wear my jacket, and I see the struggle on her face while she ponders what to do. Finally, she stops biting her bottom lip long enough to sigh. "Close your eyes."

"Why?"

"Because I'm ordering you to," she growls.

I have no good reason not to obey, but the rustle of fabric echoes in my stomach and dries up my mouth.

"Okay. I'm decent."

I blink, and the sight before me is worse than a kick in the nuts.

The hem of my jacket hugs her creamy thighs, and the V-cut shows off the lace of her bra. My treacherous cock hardens like I'm a fifteen-year-old virgin as she kicks off her fuck-me heels and lounges on the seat with her eyes closed.

I school my sight back on the road. *I can't let my mind fall down the gutter. Not ever. She's not a woman, she's a princess—and a disagreeable one at that.*

But seeing her shivering and wet, wearing nothing but lingerie and my jacket... it does things to my brain. I'll never be able to unsee *that.*

"Why are you sitting back here with me?" she asks low enough for me to wonder if she spoke at all.

A hint of shame licks my ribs as I glance at the privacy screen separating us from Jude. I should really be on the other side of that screen, discussing the attack with my second-in-command.

"You were attacked on my watch, so I'm not letting you out of my sight until we reach the castle," I finally answer, so angry with myself that I let her down earlier and that she had to deal with the flight attendant alone.

She gives a small incline of the head like my answer is reasonable enough and relaxes even more on the leather seat. "Thank you for the warm jacket, Mr. Beaumont."

ONCE THE PRINCESS is tucked safely inside her room, I meet Jasper in his office. Despite his rise in the pecking order, I refuse to suck up to him. We might be brothers, but we have nothing in common besides our damned last name.

"Here you go. One princess. Now, get me the fuck out of this assignment," I say.

The lean vampire swivels in his chair with a smug grin. "Since the princess' life has been threatened, you're being assigned to her full-time."

The fucker is going to hold every inch of his damn promotion over me, as I knew he would.

I bite the insides of my cheeks not to punch the weasel square in the jaw. "Hell to the fucking never."

He sobers up quickly, aware that, if he wasn't family, I would be tempted to pry his head off his tiny little neck. "Shush. The order comes from the king himself, at my suggestion."

I clench my fists. "Anything for the king, of course. Did you figure out what happened? Check my phone," I dump it on his deck, "and you'll see that I did send you the new schedule. And that little thumb's up in the corner...it means someone approved it from your end."

"I've already asked the tech department to look into it. Someone hacked into our system, so we're tracing the source of the leak as we speak," he grumbles, shuffling through his papers.

"What about Jason? Did he explain how his staff could have been bought off?"

"Let me worry about Jason, you've got plenty on your plate with the princess." He raises a decided brow like he's daring me to contradict him. "And Alec, no more fuck-ups."

My blood runs wild at the reproach. "You're blaming *me* for this? You sent me on this errand with no insight whatsoever and *forgot* to mention there was a specific threat, " I say, testing a hunch.

This circus wasn't a coincidence. They didn't assign me to the princess' transfer to punish me or make a point. They *knew* the princess was in danger.

"First, Eleanore slipped through your fingers, and now this... Tut-tut, you're lucky I spun this right with the king, or you would be stuck scrubbing the floors of the barracks for a couple of years."

"Tell me what you know."

Jasper leans slightly toward me, his grin all teeth and condescension. "It's above your security clearance."

I dash around his desk and imprison him in a rear-chokehold, almost wrenching him out of his seat. "I'm a senior member of the royal guard. You might have gotten the *oh-so-important* promotion, but we both know I'm your best asset. How is a threat on the life of the princess above my clearance?"

"Watch yourself, Alec. Things are changing around here," he croaks, still pleased with himself.

I release him and squint, studying the micro changes in his expression. He knows something important, that's obvious, and maybe with enough time, I can goad him into revealing his secrets.

Spinning him around so we're face to face again, I grin at my baby brother and dust off his fancy jacket. "Some things will never change, though, like the fact that I could kill you in my sleep." I whistle out of his office with a dismissive wave, knowing it'll piss him off like nothing else. "Later, *boss*."

CHAPTER 9
CASTLE
ARIELLE

I slip the jade pendant I inherited from my mother off my neck, the cold silver chain gliding along my skin. A tremor quakes my fingers as I set the rose-shaped jewel down on my dresser with a loud *thump*.

Home at last, but I almost didn't make it.

The bruise on my elbow from my tumble in the plane already faded. When the flight attendant tried to stake me, my new instincts kicked into gear. My teeth tore through her neck in no time, and though I wiped away the leftovers, the taste of her blood still thick in my mouth.

My first kill, and largely warranted, but I'm exhausted.

I sprawl on the bed and observe my new/old apartments, the size of the bedroom, walk-in closet, boudoir, and bathroom smaller than I remembered. Gone are the flashy colors and whimsical touches of childhood, the somber tones of the redecorated rooms reflecting my new position. I graze the golden accents of the bedpost with my black nails, my heart in knots.

The mind-reading incident was an isolated one so far, but my ears still buzz with the memory of Alec's unspoken words, so loud in my ears he might as well have shouted. I wonder how many provocative, petulant replies he's bit back over the years, and what was truly going through his head in the back of the car, when his eyes were so dark they would have blended with his pupils if not for the golden ring in his irises.

A quick movement in the walk-in catches my attention, and I bite back a gasp.

A girl about my age stands with her head bowed next to the concealed door of the annex. Frizzy blond curls frame her face, and the sash tied at her hips gives her handmaiden uniform some style. "Welcome home, princess. I hope you found your journey pleasant."

Pleasant like a sour grape, but the staff wouldn't have learned of my misfortune, yet, so I remain silent.

The girl shifts her weight from one foot to the other. "I'm Evangeline, one of the consort's handmaidens. She offers my services to you as a 'welcome home' present."

I blink at her a few times, wondering if I heard that phrase correctly. She's got her hands tucked at her back, her cheeks rosy and fragrant, and not one ounce of bitterness or sarcasm laces her words.

The last few years in Hadria, I got used to Jason and Emilia's ways, and they wouldn't have dreamed to speak about their staff as though they were merely presents to be handed out at will to relatives. Despite all my studies, I've forgotten some aspects of the night court's...drier sense of etiquette.

"That was very thoughtful of her. Nice to meet you, Evangeline," I say politely, mustering enough composure to forget about her warm blood for a moment.

"Can I unpack your dresses?" She moves through the room and searches for my luggage.

"I'm afraid my dresses did not travel with me. I will see my brother now. Can you—"

"They said—they told me to ask you to remain in your quarters for now. Because of the attempt on your life." Her gaze falls to the ground, the suggestion she had to relay clearly making her uncomfortable.

An attempt...how poetic and abstract.

A whiff of lavender and blood pervades the air, and my mouth waters. My teeth unsheathe in my hungry mouth, and my gaze latches on to her neck. "Will you find my first-blood? He's supposed to be here by now. His name is Leo Callas."

"Immediately, princess." With a quick bow, she scurries off, probably all too aware that she shouldn't bother a hungry newborn vampire.

The servant's door closes silently behind her—her stealth is impressive considering the feverish speed at which she left.

Dread blooms at the pit of my stomach. What if something happened to the other plane? What if Lucas and Leo got hurt? I pace the room, the grooves in the stones both familiar and eerie. Particles of dust float in the air and dry up my tongue.

I've been wracking my brains for hours, trying to determine who might have the kind of influence necessary to abduct me. The list isn't very long. There's the Zhaos, of course, the power-hungry vampire clan. We've been at war for centuries.

The vampire rebels haven't tried anything in years, but they used to cause trouble back when Ludovic took the throne, so maybe they're at it again now that he's dead.

A hot sense of relief washes over me when Leo arrives a few minutes later.

"You sent for me, princess?" he grounds out.

I jolt out of my chaise lounge, my silk robe wrapped around my frame, and dash closer to him. His familiar scent calms my nerves. "What took you so long?" I don't mean it as a reproach. More as a *where-the-hell-have-you-been-I-thought-you-were-dead* outcry.

Leo holds out his wrist, his eyes dark and dangerous.

I graze his skin with my fingers. "Wait. Not yet." I don't know if it's anger, adrenaline, fear, or a mix of the three, but I'm no longer hungry. "I'm so relieved. I thought your plane might have been attacked, too."

Deep lines crease his forehead. "You were *attacked*?"

This is not the homecoming I'd hoped for. Locked inside my room with death threats hanging over my head... I stare at him for a minute, tongue-tied, until the tightness in his shoulders eases.

"Will you hold me?" I squeak, craving his touch beyond reason.

He wraps his big arms around my frame slowly, his movements uncertain like he's trying to figure out how to connect two puzzle pieces that don't quite belong together. I hide my face in his chest, and the heat emanating from his body dizzies me. It thaws the frost. I should be ashamed of my weakness, but Leo isn't one of them. Leo is mine.

"Were you hurt?" The tremble of his voice is barely noticeable.

I shake my head and look up at him, wide-eyed. "No, but I'm scared. Why would anyone want to kidnap me? Or *kill* me?"

"I couldn't pretend to understand your world," he says in a neutral, dispassionate drawl.

The tips of my ears burn. "It said in your file that you were interested in politics. You must have an idea."

I'm still tucked in his arms, but somehow I feel the distance between us stretch and expand until he shakes his head and answers, "A change in leadership is an excellent opportunity to strike. Power dynamics are shaky when a king dies so suddenly."

"But why would they target me specifically? I have the least amount of power, and if ransom was really their end goal, they wouldn't have used lethal force." I dig my fingers into his shirt, giving him no chance to retreat. The hard muscles underneath his button-down shirt steal my breath

His green gaze latches onto my neck. "Maybe they have a different angle, one that has nothing to do with ransom or you specifically. If your brother can't protect his own sister, how can he be expected to protect his subjects?"

I dig my fingers into his chest before releasing him. "I hadn't thought of that. I knew you had something to contribute."

"Will that be all, princess?" he whispers.

The throaty request disarms me, and I want to acquiesce, but alas..."No, actually, I still need to feed."

With his chin angled to the side, he offers me his wrist again, and my stomach clenches. I need to drink because otherwise I might get too hungry and kill the next human that visits me. I thought we were finally bonding and having a real conversation, but the elusive warmth in his demeanor burned out faster than a falling star.

I hold my breath as I study his seafoam-green irises, and concentrate on the comforting rhythm of his heartbeats, wishing—hoping —to catch a glimpse of what goes on beneath the surface. I listen hard for it, in case the phenomena from before repeats itself, but Leo's mind is as silent and impregnable as his eyes.

I keep the feeding to a bare minimum, taking as little as possible, but the winces he fails to hold in wreck my soul. The bite isn't supposed to hurt that much, but I'm still so inexperienced... I promise myself to learn how to do better—and quickly—otherwise Leo and I will never get past the pain he has to endure when I feed.

Dark circles are visible under his eyes, more pronounced than they were yesterday.

I apply pressure to the bite marks to keep him from bleeding. "Have you slept at all, Leo?"

His other hand twitches at his side. "Why? I mean—yes."

"Are you sure? It's hard for the human body to get used to living at night. Are you taking your medicine?"

"Yes," he repeats stoically.

"Is there anything I can do to help? We can alter the feeding schedule until—"

He twists his arm away from my grasp. "There's no reason to alter the schedule."

The darkness in his eyes tells me this isn't just about his pain threshold.

"I know it's a big change. We'll hire our own staff, and you can make some friends." He vowed to serve me, but it's clear by now he'd rather do anything else.

"Can I go, princess?"

I click my tongue, all my attempts to ease his own transition falling on deaf ears. "Fetch me the Secrets of the Nyx, it's a leather-bound volume at the bottom of my large blue suitcase."

With a curt nod, he obeys.

He's clearly struggling, but he's being a total guy about it. No one forced him to come to the choosing ceremony. Why would he agree to pledge his life to me if he didn't want to? Plenty of islanders would have killed for the chance.

Why wouldn't he just tell me not to pick him?

Maybe he's just adjusting. Maybe he resents me for almost draining him dry. I'll ask the handmaiden to take him to the doctor if needed.

The first rays of dawn blare through the windows at my back, and my skin singes. Sunrise stings like a scorpion, with a quick, unapologetic dart, and a low, guttural hiss escapes me. I lurch to the electric blind control panel and jab the correct button until they slide down with a soft *zip*.

Ragged breaths quake my chest.

They warned me about the sun, but it hurts more than I expected. It burns deep and true, the scent of cinder thick in my nose, the flesh of my neck pulsing as it heals.

How Lucas managed to hang with me by the sea every morning baffles me.

"Princess?" Leo calls from the servant utility door. "Are you okay?"

I hold in tears and wave to the dresser. "Leave the book and go."

"As you wish."

I stare at the wall until he leaves, but inside, I'm shaking. Red-stained tears flow down my cheeks. What good does it do me to be a vampire princess if I have to remain locked inside my room?

64

Leo hates me, and my family's enemies want me dead. My own body feels foreign, my senses wild and unfamiliar. They said I would feel better, stronger, but they failed to mention the caveats. Am I really still *Ari* with all this pent-up...violence inside me? Am I doomed to be one of these ill-fated vampires who can't ever walk in sunlight again?

All these new sensations and hormones are driving me crazy, worse than puberty—and that's saying something.

My gaze latches on to the book I requested, and I snatch it off the dresser, eager to recheck a few passages on the powers afforded to only some of Nyx's children. If memory serves right, mind-reading should be right at the end of the chapter on telepathy.

CHAPTER 10
UPSTAIRS, DOWNSTAIRS
LEO

"Nice digs. It's twice as big as mine." Quentin says from the comfort of my bed.

The door leading to the princess' room closes behind me, masked in the tapestries, and I consider the intruder with a cramped jaw. First-bloods live in what they call an annex, a connecting room to their master's apartments that we can also exit from the other side if we need to travel to the servant's hall without bothering the bloodsuckers. The princess' status allows me the perk of also having a private bathroom.

Arielle just went to bed, and I'd hoped for a bit of peace and quiet —something I can't take for granted anymore. I exhale loudly and tug on my sleeve, masking the marks her teeth left in my wrist. The pads of my fingers are numb and cold, and though I want to tell Quentin to fuck off and let me curl up in a ball on my bed, I can't quite find the energy to do it.

Quentin's face darkens. "Hey, don't worry man, the feeding part becomes a lot more fun after a while. Let me wrap it up for you." He rummages below the bathroom sink and comes back with the special first-aid kit Jean presented to me on my first day.

With a wince, he bandages the mess she made on my arm. "The first week or so is the worst. They learn to bite with more finesse after that."

I press my lips together. "Why were you waiting in my room?"

He taps his hand gently to his forehead. "I forgot to tell you. Since we're both new at court, Evangeline volunteered to show us around. She should fetch us any minute now."

I open my mouth to refuse, but instead blurt out, "How did you know the princess was in danger?"

Quentin freezes. "Danger? I never said the princess was in danger."

"You told me I might survive her." I watch his face for tells.

The dude drops his gaze to the floor like a five year old caught with his face full of chocolate. "I didn't know she was—I just over-heard something."

I blink at him a few times, but he doesn't elaborate. "Are you really going to wait for me to ask? What the fuck did you overhear?"

"I was kissing a nice kitchen maid in the food pantry the other night, and I heard Jason Delacroix speaking on the phone. He was using his polite, ceremonious voice. He said to the person on the other end of the line that he felt uncomfortable lying to the princess. That she should know she's in danger."

My brows pull together. "Why didn't you tell anyone?"

"I don't want any trouble, mate. Besides, he could have been talking about anything." His forehead creases. "I thought you didn't like the girl?"

Eyes falling to the ground, I scratch the tip of my shoe on the carpet. "I don't want her to be *murdered*."

"I don't get you man. One minute you bite my face off for talking casually about our employers, and the next you have a fit about protecting the princess."

"I'm not protecting her, I'm—"

A quiet knock on the door startles us both, and we exchange a meaningful glance. I might not trust Quentin completely, but I do trust his apparent inability to tell a lie. And he's right, we shouldn't stick our necks out because of a one-off sentence he overheard while he was fucking a maid.

Quentin swings open the door leading to the hallway and leans on the doorframe. "Hey, beautiful."

Evangeline wrinkles her nose. "Ready for a stroll around the castle?"

She's only a handmaiden, which apparently means she's below us, but she doesn't lack wits or confidence as she shows us around. Blond curls bounce around her face, her easy smile and casual manners putting me at ease.

"It's not all cold bricks and dimly lit corridors. A big portion of the castle has been renovated to reflect the new trends. The oldest foundations date back to the 1500s. The whole castle was designed with most windows facing north, to avoid as much direct sunlight as possible." Evangeline points to a big chandelier hanging above our heads. "Major renovations were done in the 1920s to pass electric wiring and redo the whole sanitation system. The modern wing was added in the 2000s after Ludovic's wedding, with a complete redo of the moon room and the gardens. The east, west, and south-facing windows now have top-of-the-line electric blinds." She presses on a remote to show us the effect.

Heavily tinted blinds glide down to cover the windows.

Goosebumps riddle my arms. "Sunlight can't kill them, right?"

Quentin snickers. "My man Leo has got his mythos crossed with Hollywood movies. It's not a Dracula fortress, mate. More like Downton Abbey but with plasma screen TVs."

"The modern wing is mainly reserved for the king and his family, so we can't visit. Look, the princess was just a baby here." Evangeline nudges my arm and points to an old portrait of the Delacroix family.

"You're quite the historian," Quentin says with a pleasant smile.

"I read about it in the first-blood diaries. The first-blood to the old king—that's what we call the princess' father—died a few years ago, but she was quite the storyteller."

"Could I read it?" I ask.

She skims my arm. "Sure. I'll bring it to you tonight. Now, if you'll excuse me, gentlemen, I have work to do."

Quentin kisses her hand before she leaves, and I wave goodbye awkwardly.

"Cheer up, Leo. This job comes with perks."

Job? Perks? It's like we're chatting about health benefits and retirement funds instead of bloodshed and slavery. I serve him an icy glare.

"Come on, man. That gorgeous girl touched your arm five times during the tour."

I arch a brow, pondering his statement. I guess she did, but I was too busy sulking to notice.

"Be smart. She's the queen's handmaiden. That kind of connection could come in handy."

My gaze falls to the wound on my wrist, and all I can think about is the princess' dark blue eyes. She's made to attract, her beauty meant to lure innocent victims into her cold, deadly embrace. And her smell...pomegranates and sunshine, like the island I lost forever.

I lied to her. I haven't been sleeping at all.

All I see when I close my eyes are her red lips pressed on my pulse point, her pink tongue licking the blood off the wound. Her content gasps ring in my ears whenever I try to rest...

Before I can process another thought, my fist shatters the big vase in the middle of the sitting room. Broken pieces of crystal scatter across the marble floor, tinkling like diamonds on ice.

Quentin frowns and puts his hands in front him. "What's wrong with you, man?"

"Wrong with me? What's wrong with *you*? We're vampire slaves, and you're talking about making connections like we just landed a corporate job."

He puffs his chest. "They suck our blood, so what? We get to be part of their lives, of their story. We don't have to pay bills or bother with human problems. We get to boss around a bunch of people and fuck pretty girls."

"What about freedom? We're stuck with them until we die."

A grimace deforms the pretty boy's face. "Who's free, really? All normals are slaves to their jobs. Fine, we don't get many vacation days, but we don't have to cook or empty the dishwasher or do laundry. We're personal assistants to immortal billionaires."

"Whatever, *mate*." I huff and bury my hands in my pockets. Quentin is smitten by the lifestyle, and it sickens me.

"Please, drop that martyr routine, already. You volunteered for this. You vowed you were doing it of your own free will."

I inch closer to him. "I had no choice. Don't talk about things you don't understand."

"You made a choice Leo. Nobody forced you back on the island. Nobody dragged your ass to the choosing ceremony. It might not have been an easy one, maybe fate forced your hand, but it was a choice. Stop being a baby and own it."

A tall, short-haired woman appears at the top of the stairs and interrupts our argument. "I'm Sabina, First-Blood to the queen, and the one responsible for your court training. Come with me, please."

Sabina's bossy French accent scrapes my ears, but I jump at the opportunity to shut Quentin up and fall into step with her. The vampire groupie mumbles a gruff goodbye as the more somber newcomer guides me back to the princess' apartments through the annex.

She holds her black clipboard close to her chest. "I heard you were twenty-nine."

"Yeah."

"Hm."

The bedroom door is closed, so the princess is sleeping.

Sabina points to the back of the walk-in closet. A small nook that was previously vacant now holds a massage table, and a black woman lies upon it, naked.

What the—

"Etiquette is tomorrow. Today is a refresher course on how to give a nice massage. The princess also required a yoga instructor, but I figured we could hire someone from the village," Sabina says.

Blood buzzes in my ears. "Why can't we hire a massage therapist, too?"

"Because you studied physical therapy for two years. You should be able to handle a massage. Besides, the princess will be sensitive to the scent of strangers for a while, and yoga isn't as intimate."

Does everyone here have my resume or something?

Sabina taps her pen to the girl's exposed butt. "Cheryl here volunteered to be your practice run."

"I couldn't pass up on that." The girl winks, a thin gold line applied over her long lashes.

"Will I learn to paint nails, too?" I ask dryly.

Sabina scribbles a few words on her clipboard. "If you want to."

These people don't understand the concept of sarcasm. *Fuck me.*

CHAPTER II
WHAT A GIRL WANTS
ARIELLE

T he evening after the attack, I swing open my bedroom door after sundown and almost ram into Alec Beaumont. I just fed on Leo, his delectable blood still warm in my stomach, but the sight of the assassin ruins my cheery mood.

"What are you still doing here?" I shout out, startled.

The assassin stares blankly ahead, hands linked at his front, his typical I'm-well-trained-but-also-overqualified-for-this-job stance. "I'm your new personal bodyguard. The king ordered it."

A big frown twists my face. "Take me to my brother."

"You won't change his mind about this. Believe me, I tried."

I sink my nails inside my palms and force my voice to remain even and congenial. "Believe *me*, Mr. Beaumont. I have more important things to discuss with the king than your assignment."

He snickers under his breath. "After you, Lucky."

I bite back a growl. I won't give him the satisfaction of knowing how much he annoys me. It would just goad him to taunt me more. The queen's younger brother comes to mind at the thought. Sebastian Chastain was every bit as cocky and obnoxious as Alec, using the years he had over me to belittle my opinions.

Still...I keep close tabs on Alec from the corner of my eyes, and listen for a snarky, loose thought.

Mind-reading isn't exactly a common side-effect of the Nightfall, so I decided not to bring it up until it happens again. According to all my books, powers of this sort are extremely rare. And they usually skip a generation...

Who knows, maybe Beaumont merely used his telepathic abilities to answer me by mistake. Our best soldiers are well-trained in the quiet art of mind-language, and he might have accidentally projected his thoughts.

Once we enter the royal office, Alec sidesteps to stand guard next to the door, clasping both hands in front of himself again.

Victor is sitting at his desk at the back of the room, the fabric of his tuxedo glimmers with a rich swirl of bronze and gold as he stands to greet me.

I curtsy. "Victor. I mean—my king."

He grabs my hands and squeezes them. "Ari. You've grown so much."

He hugs me, and I close my eyes. The scent of leather and peppermint linger in my nose, as potent as they were when my father held me in his arms, and Victor releases me too quickly.

"I'm so glad you went through your Nightfall in time to attend the coronation tomorrow. I was appalled when I heard about the attack. I'm glad to see it didn't steal your beautiful smile." He returns to his chair and motions for me to sit in front of him.

"Am I in danger? Is that why—" I motion discreetly to Alec.

Victor lowers his voice. "We are investigating the matter. You shouldn't worry too much about it. It's standard for a princess to have a bodyguard. Especially now when we have so many visitors around for the coronation."

"But Alec Beaumont?" I whisper the name as quietly as I can.

"I know the circumstances of the attack might have rattled you, but he's the best. Truly."

I want to argue, but the way Victor stares directly into my eyes tightens my throat.

The corners of his mouth quirk. "You look even more like Mother than you did when you were little."

I play with my fingers, eyes cast down. "Thank you. I was hoping... I want to pay my respect to our late brother."

"Of course. Come with me." He stands up and offers me his arm.

I don't really want to see where Ludovic was laid to rest, but I'm eager to escape Alec's scrutiny and speak a little more with Victor in private.

Humidity thickens over the walls as we make our way down to the family crypt. Torches cast a warm light over the silhouettes of our fallen monarchs, Ludovic's bronze statue standing next to Mother's and Father's, though my father's corpse was lost at sea. Ludovic's handsome face is even more beautiful in death, no spiel flowing from his mouth.

"Such a shame," I lie.

Victor squeezes my arm. "He never should have married that she-demon."

"He should have been kinder." I try hard not to dwell on Mother's face. I will come back later, alone, and cry my heart out. Victor, Genevieve... no one has to tell me how similar we look. I see it everyday in the mirror.

She shouldn't have been buried here. Her funeral should have taken place on Hadria, like in the old days, but Ludovic was adamant, and my grievances went unheard, as always.

I turn back to Victor. "I heard Adele is expecting again."

A genuine smile glazes his lips. "She is."

"Congratulations."

He tugs me back toward the stairs. "You haven't seen your nephew in a while."

"He must be so big now. Are you ready for the coronation?"

The conversation drifts away from death to lighter subjects. We talk about the menu for tomorrow and exchange pleasantries about my time on the island and his new responsibilities. I've always preferred Victor to Ludovic, but since the latter was a psychopath, he wasn't that hard to beat.

My mind wanders off before we're done, flying back to the investigation. I can't shake the feeling that Victor knows more than he lets on. If my flesh and blood was attacked the day before my coronation, I'd have my best guys on it. I wouldn't be talking about wine choices. I'd want answers.

Which means Victor already has them.

I thought my transformation meant that I'd finally be heard, that my opinions would matter, that I wouldn't be so easily dismissed. But becoming a vampire only changed my physical abilities and my diet.

After we say goodbye, I walk back to the main hall. The midnight blue tapestries on the walls of the round stairwell shimmer on both sides, the gold accents distracting me from the path, and I almost trip over my heels. The scents of pork guts, garlic, and sage waft in from the kitchens below, dizzying me, and the distant voices and footsteps of servants and government officials blur together as though I'm underwater. Alec shadows me, silent and discreet as a ghost.

His presence behind me brings a sense of foreboding. My instincts are telling me to run from older, more powerful predators, and my blood flows faster, the feeling so different from when I was human. When a vampire's blood races, the heart doesn't beat faster, but it aches. I feel...trapped.

Dark spots dance in front of my eyes when we get to the corridor leading to the queen's apartments. I would run through here as a child when I'd had a nightmare and barge through my mother's door only to jump into the huge bed at the back of the suite.

This is where the royal guard snatched me in his arm the night she—

"Are you okay, princess?" Alec whispers softly behind me.

I pick up the pace, shaking my head forcefully to erase the memories threatening to surface. "I'm fine."

In the main parlor, a place where the highest-ranking officers of the court can gather in peace, I spot a familiar face, and the tightness in my chest recedes.

Prime minister Peter Chastain is standing next to the fireplace, chatting with two men I don't know, a few other government officials, and their guests exchanging quips over tea and biscuits on the big sofas.

Peter's voice is clear and deep as he interrupts his conversation to greet me. "Princess. You are a sight for sore eyes."

I bite the insides of my cheeks. Between his light brown hair, gorgeous eyes, and square jaw, Peter Chastain is a work of art, but all of that pales in comparison to his charisma.

A blue satin suit hugs his lithe frame, and I can't help but stare as I offer him a respectful nod. "Prime Minister Chastain."

"Ah, princess, I wish you would start calling me Peter." He covers my hands with his. "My condolences for your brother's passing."

My skin tingles all over. "Thank you."

His companion bows. "You're the spitting image of your mother, your highness. It's a privilege to meet you. I'm Axel Brooks."

I keep my gaze firmly planted on Peter. "Your daughter is in confinement, I hear?" My voice is higher and more melodic than usual.

"She should grace us with a second heir any day now." He lets my hands go, still smiling, and I can't help but smile back.

In a sea of old, patronizing vampires, Peter always stood out. When he looked at me, it felt as though I was the only person in the room, and he actually listened to my answers when he asked a question. He was the only one who bothered to ask for my opinion when I was a bloodling.

My whole body vibrates in excitement at finally meeting him as an adult instead of a child he humors with conversation.

Lucas erupts into the hall, breathless, and hurries in my direction. He raises a hand toward my arm, but catches himself in time, and lets it fall by his side. "Good evening, princess."

"Excuse me, but I have a meeting in a few minutes. Nice to see you again, Lord Pereira." Peter leaves us, and I can't help but follow his movements until he disappears from view.

Damn Chastain men and their impossible charm.

Lucas inches closer. "You kept your blue eyes."

"Yes." A few of the men present sneak glances at us, and goosebumps prickle my neck. "It's good to see you, Lord Pereira."

Lucas' gaze turns analytical as he notices our audience. "It's an honor to be here for the coronation," he says loudly before whispering, "Can I come to your room? I heard about the attack."

My chest cramps at the dark expression on his face. "Meet me there in half an hour, I still have to approve my new staff."

With a small nod, he acknowledges my answer and orders a cup of tea from the butler.

I wonder what Peter's meeting was about. I should have asked him instead of staring at his eyelashes. I should have asked about the attack instead of blabbering about his daughter giving birth.

God, he must think I'm an idiot.

Beating myself inwardly for losing my cool, I walk to the library where Leo has gathered the candidates for my staff. Most of them already work for the night court and are looking for a promotion, so I'm sure he had no trouble finding capable help.

Evangeline hops down from the mahogany table she's sitting on as soon as she sees me coming, but it's too late. I've seen her slouch. Blood floods to her cheeks as I walk to the front of the room.

Five humans form a line next to my first-blood, his new haircut giving him a severe edge. They all curtsy at my arrival.

"I find you all in good hands, I hope?" I say.

They all answer, "Yes, your majesty," in perfect synchrony.

I turn to Leo. "Anything you wanted to run by me?"

"They are all more than qualified for the job, though I figured you might like to taste the food. I asked the *patissier* to prepare your favorite dessert, lemon cake."

A man with a white apron approaches, holding a plate, but my nose wrinkles when my gaze lands on the triangular piece of cake he's offering.

"I think that from now on, I'll be more of a red-velvet girl, with o-negative instead of cherry."

That gets me a few polite laughs from the crowd, but Leo remains as stoic as a statue.

"Anything else?" I skim the rest of the staff. The two new hand-maids wear bland servant uniforms, their hearts fluttering like hummingbird wings. They're either absolutely terrified—or superbly excited—to get the job. I hope it's the latter.

I stop in front of the thirty-something woman at the end of the line. Red peep-toe heels add a splash of color to her feet, and a sumptuous tailored jacket with black satin lapels wraps her frame. Professional but sexy. Big white glasses are perched atop her round nose, and her crisp, red lipstick matches her shoes. "I want that outfit. You're the personal shopper?"

The girl doesn't bat an eye. "Yes, princess. I'm Bella."

"Nice choice, Mr. Callas."

He averts his gaze, hands tucked behind his back.

I stare at him, crestfallen. What am I supposed to do if the simplest of praises rubs him the wrong way?

RIGHT ON SCHEDULE, a quiet knock echoes from my bedroom door. "Your highness, Lord Pereira is asking to see you," Alec announces from the other side, his voice perfectly professional.

"Let him in, Mr. Beaumont." I stretch on the chaise lounge, snap my book shut, and put it aside as Lucas inches inside.

My friend glances around my rooms with his arms tucked at his sides the way one might observe an outlandish, new land. Judging by the frown on his face, the new colors are probably not to his taste. "Hello, princess."

I roll my eyes at him. "Come on, we're alone now." I motion for him to sit on the stool right in front of me. "Come sit. I'm excited to see you."

He shakes out his hands as he sits, his gaze now solely focused on me. "What happened yesterday? I heard the most gruesome rumors."

Over the next half an hour, I offer him a play by play of the plane ride and circumstances that led to the attack, the frown on his face gradually deepening.

"Sounds like your bodyguard is incompetent—or crooked," he whispers low enough for Alec not to hear.

"No, I don't think he's to blame, really." I'm not sure why I'm defending him, other than my intuition tells me that if Alec had been anybody else, I'd be in enemies' hands right now—or dead.

"You could have been killed." The wind of his breath caresses my cheek, and his gaze flicks to my lips.

"I'm a vampire now, I can defend myself." I add a dazzle of bravado to my voice and inch closer, eager to find out exactly how different his kiss will taste now that we're on equal footing.

Suddenly, Lucas stands and side steps away from me, his palms spread on each side of him. "Well...I have to go, or I'll be late for my meeting."

What the hell?

I cock my head to the side, wondering why he's so shifty all of a sudden—and why he changed his mind about kissing me again. "Meeting?"

"Not a meeting... I—I've been invited to dinner."

"By whom?"

"Your brother."

My eyes narrow. He keeps his cards close to the vest, making me ask for details instead of supplying them, and that's unlike him. "You have an audience with the king? Why?"

"I don't know." He shifts his weight from one foot to the other.

I raise a conspiratorial brow at him, smiling despite the queasiness in my stomach. "You'll tell me all about it tomorrow at the ceremony?"

"You bet," he cracks nervously.

With a sigh, I resist the urge to riddle him with questions. Lucas doesn't know Victor very well. It must be pretty nerve-wracking for him to be summoned by the king. "Let's walk together. I'll escort you over to the king's wing and take a stroll through the gardens on my way back." I offer him my arm, and he takes it without much resistance.

Maybe if I catch a glimpse of who else was invited to this meeting, I can figure out what it's about.

CHAPTER 12

MASTER OF WAR

ALEC

The secluded royal gardens separate the princess' apartments from the king and queen's wings. It is one of the most secure areas in the kingdom, and allows the royal family—and highest-ranking members of government—safety and privacy at all hours of the day.

People like me don't trust open spaces as much as the comfort provided by a well-guarded building, but this is the exception. Soldiers posted at the corners of the estate prevent surveillance drones—or anything of the sort—from preying on the royal family.

It's a most private space, reserved for a handful of people, and my spine stiffens when I spot my brother, Garret, sitting on the edge of the fountain in the middle of the courtyard with Sabina, the queen consort's first-blood.

"Hey, Alec." He waves from his seat causally, as though he belongs in this elitist inner sanctum.

His rise in the ranks might entitle him to hang out here, but my brother detests flowers and plants, which makes me doubt his motives. I haven't seen him since my return, and his new midnight-blue uniform possesses one too many embroideries. When Jude texted me that Garrett now commanded our army, I didn't totally believe it.

He probably has a room on the same floor as the prime minister, but no uniform or title could ever convince me that he's able to put someone else's interest ahead of his own.

Sabina stops writing on her clipboard and licks her lips as the princess and I draw near, her butt sliding away from Garrett a few inches along the rim of the fountain. I wonder what leading an army has to do with her, but I shouldn't be surprised. Garrett flirts with all the girls.

I guess we have that one flaw in common.

Arielle slows down, one hand clenched around the skirt of her dress. "Mr. Beaumont. Are you going to introduce me to your friend?"

As if on cue, the bastard walks over to us and kisses the back of her hand as he bows. "Garrett Beaumont, your majesty. I hope my little brother didn't give you too many reasons to hate our family. I know first-hand how difficult he can be."

The princess fucking laughs, her eyes beaming. "I hear you've been made Master of War. Congratulations, Sir Beaumont."

He gives her a quick nod, his voice slick as honey. "It's an honor to serve your family, your highness."

"Are our soldiers holding strong?"

Garrett flashes his signature wolfish grin. "We'll make the Zhaos spit out bile."

"It was nice to meet you, Sir Beaumont. Keep up the good work."

My brother brings an arm to his chest to salute her, and she prances away from us. I move to follow, but he puts himself in my way.

"She's got more spirit than Victor," he says with a wistful smile.

I follow the princess' movements with my eyes, annoyed by the intrusion. We might be in the most secure area of the castle, but that's no reason to botch my duties. "I've got to go."

"Wait." He braces his hand on my shoulder to stop me from leaving. "This assignment is a slap in the face, but don't let the opportunity go to waste. You have unparalleled access to the princess. Stop alienating her and build a relationship."

"How do you know if I'm alienating her?"

"Because I know you, Alec."

The sharp glint in his eyes gives me pause. Of the three of us, Garrett has always had the best grasp on politics. Shrewd diplomacy, information manipulation, and knowing exactly where your enemy is vulnerable are amongst his best—and worse—qualities.

I lick my lips. "Are you saying I should *spy* on the princess? Is that why you're having a midnight *chat* with the queen consort's first-blood?"

He shrugs. "Don't put words in my mouth. Having the princess on your side is just smart."

"I've got to go, *sir*." I scoff out the last part, telegraphing exactly how empty his new title actually is.

Garrett grows a shade whiter, the gentle carefreeness erased from his face, but he lets me go.

He might be allowed to lurk in the royal gardens, but he'll always be held apart. We're not blue-blooded enough for the Lords to really let us into their fancy little circle, and if my brother has forgotten that, he'll soon be reminded. We're only soldiers to them, and soldiers are made to follow orders, not debate them.

I move to catch up to my charge before she steps under the balcony.

A mysterious smile glazes her lips. "Your brother is nice."

"My brother is a suck-up," I snap, unable to stop myself.

"No one could accuse *you* of that, Mr. Beaumont."

"I pride myself in keeping it real."

She shoots me a glance over her shoulder. Her blue eyes gleam with mischief, and she laughs, but the sound isn't sarcastic. I'm taken aback by her reaction...and the unfamiliar squeeze in my gut at the joyous, melodic sound.

Unparalleled access to the princess.

My brother might see it as an opportunity to befriend a royal and influence her decisions, but his words planted a totally different scenario in my mind. If I'm not careful, I'll give the new king a scandalous reason to court-martial my sorry ass.

THE NEXT NIGHT brings an entirely new world of pain as the coronation gets underway. Pompous traditions drain the life out of me, and working security for the event of the century brought its load of challenges. I'm already exhausted by the time I put on my most regal uniform.

White roses garnish the banisters of the main hall, the freshly cut flowers painted with freckles of blood. Exotic fragrances waft through the air, and a red and gold carpet leads the way to the underground chapel where the ceremony will take place.

Jasper joins me on the mezzanine overlooking the entrance hall. "Shouldn't you be with the princess?"

"She's with the king. They asked for privacy."

He sniffs the closest bouquet of roses and picks a few stems out of the bunch. "Blood from all over the world. A teenage girl from Bali. An elderly man from San Francisco. A strong lad from Benin... Humanity will never stop longing for us."

"Ugh. They were merely tourists who didn't know what they were walking into," I grumble.

"Still...how wild is it that they keep coming, even though we kill so many of them?"

Garrett joins us on the landing and squints at me. "Where were you this afternoon? I couldn't find you."

They're both wearing the family's colors—blue and white— while I'm adorned in red and black.

I clear my throat. "I was investigating the attack on the princess." With little success, but I keep that part to myself.

Jasper grins. "Don't be silly, brother. We both know you're not as loyal to the crown as you appear."

My eyes narrow. What is he implying?

"You did good, Alec, when you let Eleanor escape," Garrett says. "Victor will chase his own tail looking for her while I deal with the Zhaos as I see fit."

His words fall over me like snowflakes, cold and numbing. For better or worse, my brothers know me better than anyone, and there's no use pretending. They'd never believe that I lost a fight against Elle or her werewolves without taking at least one of them down. The only thing uncertain is how they plan to use that information to their advantage.

I straighten the sleeves of my jacket. "I didn't do it for you."

Jasper pats my back. "Whatever you need to tell yourself. A special tribunal will be held tomorrow, and I'll make sure you get a chance to explain your failure without too much prodding."

I crack a smile. "Go to hell."

"Aren't you sick of being ordered around? For centuries we Beaumonts have served the crown faithfully only to be given scraps," Jasper chimes.

"Ludovic made Garrett Master of War before he died. That's not *scraps*," I say.

Jasper snickers, the sound dry and ugly. "He should have been the new prime minister, but Victor insisted on keeping Peter fucking Chastain, and now the bastard is in charge. Victor will never grow enough balls to stand up to him."

Garrett nods. "Victor turns up his nose at us. Look at you. You're the stealthiest assassin at his disposal, and he's got you babysitting the princess."

My eyes wrinkle. "What are you talking about? Jasper is the one who put me up to this."

"I had no choice about that. Victor was adamant," Jasper says quietly.

Interesting... he certainly didn't want to admit he'd been forced to assign me to her, even going so far as to pretend it was his idea.

Garrett motions to Jasper with his palm up, emphasizing the fact that he agrees with him. "Yes, exactly! Peter put Victor up to it. If you were a proper soldier, I would have authority over you. I could make you general."

"Imagine that," I crack.

"Oh—stop with the attitude," Jasper adds. "I admit, guarding the princess is below your pay grade, even if it's only for a few weeks. Once she's off to Brazil, you can—"

All the saliva dries from my mouth. "The king is marrying her off to Felipe Pereira?"

"Yes. We need his help with the war. He's got eyes and ears in the Zhaos' Court," Garrett says.

"And he asked for the princess' hand in return?"

"Wouldn't you? I mean—I'd heard the rumors, but that girl is a vampire's wet dream..." Jasper trails off.

All my life, I've tried and failed to evade my siblings, and it seems today is no exception. I excuse myself under the guise of checking on the princess, but I slip inside the bathroom and splash water on my face. Nyx be damned, I really wish I'd been an only child. They're going to use what they know about Elle's escape to reel me into whatever plan they have in motion.

An old fucker like Pereira shouldn't be allowed to marry our princess, it's as simple as that. I wait a few minutes before going back out, knowing they'll allow the guests in soon and that I'll need to be by the princess' side when they do.

My brothers are no longer stalking the entrance of the chapel as I return, government officials filtering inside for the ceremony.

A voice I haven't heard in years booms from the shadow of the alcove. "Well, isn't it my favorite Beaumont?"

Oh, hell. I squint at the apparition.

The redhead vampire pushes himself off the wall and strolls in my direction.

"Welcome back, Sebastian. Should I arrest you right now, or would you prefer to be wrestled out of the chapel in front of everyone?"

Funny thing is, I'm actually serious. Both options work for me, but I could deal with a little drama if he preferred to ruffle a few feathers. Could be interesting.

He straightens my ceremonial scarf with a wink. "It's Lord Chastain to you. And I'm not trespassing. Victor granted me a reprieve on my sentence."

The corners of my mouth quirk. *Hell yeah.* "My Lord, what brings you back to France? I thought we were a bunch of boring, old-fashioned necrophiles."

"The bogeyman is dead. It was time to mend fences with the fam." He salutes me with two fingers and heads inside the chapel.

Sebastian's last words to Ludovic were pretty much the highpoint of the last decade. Despite his obnoxiousness, you had to admire the guile of the kid. A newborn vamp telling the vilest vampire king in centuries to go fuck himself...it was a sight to see.

If he hadn't been a Chastain, and the prime minister's only son, his skull would have been welded to the throne.

CHAPTER 13
IN A CROWN
ARIELLE

The string quartet's delightful rendition of "Swan Lake" lures me from the chapel into the ballroom, the celebratory ball only just beginning. Chandeliers twinkle above our heads as the guests filter in, in stark contrast with the dark, mysterious atmosphere of the chapel. Alec nips at my heels, the pressure of his gaze on my back almost as vivid as a graze.

The royal guard was sitting behind me during the coronation, and yet his piercing eyes were more interested in watching *me* than his new king. After riddling the nape of my neck with goosebumps for the first half of the ceremony, he spent the next hour studying my crown of braids like it was a marvel of modern engineering, and even adjusted a loose clip in my hair.

Now that it's over, I should scold him for touching me, but I can't bring myself to do it. The soft gesture chased away the boredom, preventing me from nodding off to sleep.

Exotic flavors of human blood tickle my gums, the delicacies like catnip to my newborn vampire senses. Hemoglobin chocolate cake, A-negative cherries...I decide to steer clear of the hors d'oeuvres table altogether. I'm not here to stuff my face and need to keep my wits about me, not argue with my bodyguard in front of the whole court.

I grab a flute of champagne from an offered tray to wash off the tantalizing aromas from my mouth and weave through the crowd to find Lucas.

My friend is standing alone near the bar, stuck between the dance floor and the wall of courtiers chatting next to the banquet tables. The crowd parts for me as I head over to him.

"Hey," I offer him a small smile. "I missed you in the first row. I saved a seat for you. Why didn't you come?"

"Don't be ridiculous, I couldn't sit with you," he answers quietly.

I eye him up and down, only now noticing the sunken dark circles under his eyes. "What happened yesterday during dinner? You look like you haven't slept at all."

"Oh, it was lovely," he says, snapping out of whatever miserable gutter his mind was stuck in. "Your brother is very wise and generous."

"Are you sure nothing happened?" I say, surprised by the formality of his answer. The dancers can't possibly be listening to our conversation, and the people sitting at the tables are all chatting loudly. Unless Lucas is worried about Alec... "Will you go and fetch me a glass of wine, Mr. Beaumont?"

Alec opens his mouth, and I'm sure he's about to refuse, but he forces his jaw closed and obeys with a curt nod.

I smile from ear-to-ear, turning back to Lucas. "We can speak freely now."

"No, really. Nothing happened. I just didn't sleep very well. Ate too much," he adds with a guilty wince, patting his stomach discreetly.

"Looks like you've finally outgrown those clunky pigtails, Lil' Bit."

The familiar voice freezes both of us into silence, and my teeth grit together, my entire body stiffening as though it's bracing itself for impact.

Sebastian Chastain, my childhood bully and tormentor, adjusts his tie, his garnet eyes fixed on the diamond necklace wrapped around my neck as he moves closer.

I can't evade him, so I school my sight firmly on the dance floor and sip on my champagne. I haven't seen the bastard in years, and I do not want to notice all the small changes in him or let my gaze roam over the new shape of his body. Once upon a time, I thought our destinies were intwined, but I'm better off without him, regardless of what my mother used to say.

Sebastian nudges Lucas's shoulder with his fist. "Lulu, how are you?"

Lucas jumps backward, his mouth twisted in a bitter pout. "Don't call me that."

Sebastian steps all the way into my bubble, not sparing Lucas another look. The light hits his auburn hair just right, and my heart gives a nostalgic squeeze. Sebastian always looked like he was sculpted in fire, and his Nightfall certainly didn't strip that away from him.

"Dance with me, Ari." He offers me his hand, and I glance around the room.

While I would love nothing more than to refuse Sebastian, I do not want to disrespect the queen, so I discard my flute on a waiter's tray and take her brother's hand.

Sebastian's gaze slides down my cleavage, and a thrill shoots up my spine. He once called me an ugly bloodling, and it's empowering to have this effect on him now. As empty as it is, I crave the vindication it delivers.

He whisks me to the dance floor and pulls me close. "I bet Hadria was exceptionally boring without me."

"It was nice to be respected, for a change."

"Ah! Is that what you truly crave? Respect?" His palm presses hard on my lower back as he leans in my ear. "Do you remember your fourteenth birthday?"

I ignore the wild *boom* in my demon heart and force myself to appear bored. "How can I forget? You set fire to my dress."

While I was still in it.

His heated gaze flicks to my lips. "You admitted something that day, between curses and sobs."

"Yes. Crazy how after that, my crush on you literally went up in *smoke*."

A meaningless, teenage crush. I will not deny it because he would see right through me. A few too many diaries started and ended with hearts containing his name, but I'm older now. I see his rebel vibe for what it is: a plea for attention.

His warm chuckle riddles my skin with goosebumps. "I missed your sharp wit."

"I didn't think of you at all."

His eyes darken, calling my bluff. "No? Not even on Christmas?"

Despite my best efforts not to react, my teeth grit together. Christmas... the night he robbed me of my first kiss and broke my heart. To this day, snowflakes and candy canes still set me on edge. When we got to Hadria and discovered he'd already transitioned, Lucas and I spent months gossiping about his antics, bound together in our grim fascination for the bully that didn't want to play by the rules.

"You left for Hadria on Christmas, I think? Or was it right after? I can't remember," I say, playing dumb.

He cups the side of my face, grinning like he's delighted by my answer—and believes none of it. "Lie to the night court, Lil' Bit, but you don't have to pretend with me." His hand wanders dangerously close to my ass. "Our legacy will not allow us to be meek. The blood you feasted on in that chamber and every night since throbs in your veins, calling for sin and violence. I remember how maddening it was the first week. The dull pounding in my head would not relent, and I was dying to drain a room full of slaves, drag their hot skin against mine, and fuck their brains out," a cunning smile glazes his lips as he hesitates, "—though not necessarily in that order."

Lust and need flutter in my stomach. "I'm not a mindless animal."

"You're a Delacroix." He presses me closer, way too close not to raise eyebrows, his rushed breaths caressing the shell of my ear. "Don't let your stubborn brother sell you off to Brazil."

My shoulders stiffen. "What do you mean?"

He clicks his tongue. "They didn't tell you. Typical." He rests his cheek against mine, and my already cold blood freezes in my veins. "The king already accepted a proposal in your name."

A big frown overpowers my crafted mask of indifference. "But…" My gaze darts to Lucas. "Not Lucas, surely."

"Felipe Pereira," Sebastian whispers.

Adrenaline raises my voice a few octaves. "You're mistaken."

"Don't shoot the messenger. They act as though it's a done deal, and I thought they'd at least have told you before making it official."

I do not trust the compassionate bend of his brow. Knowing him as I do, he's probably delighted to be the bearer of bad news. With a growl, I push him off of me and scurry over to Lucas who's still standing on the edge of the dance floor.

"Did you know?" I bark at my friend. "Is that what your *meeting* was about?"

He takes both my hands in his, his gaze soft and apologetic. "Yes. Victor wants me to escort you to Brazil, Ari."

"What?" The room starts to spin, the candlelights blurry and hypnotic.

"Victor decided to marry you to my uncle. This is about the Zhaos. They're sniffing around Europe, and an unbreakable alliance with my family is exactly what your brother needs to keep the peace."

"But he *can't*." Blood thumps away my denial.

He can. And he will.

Because what the king wants, the king gets, and what a princess needs gets shot to hell.

I sink my nails in my palms and rush past Sebastian to the champagne fountain. If I had run to the exit, the eyes of my fellow vampires would have zeroed-in on me, but predators don't hone in on women rushing for champagne. I fill a flute to the brim, counting down from twenty, and discreetly discard it on the table.

Just as I'm about to veer in the direction of the bathroom, a familiar, crystal-clear greeting reaches my ear.

"Hey, Ari."

I spin around and curtsy to my queen. "Your highness."

The bells in her voice remind me of a different time, when she thought she'd never be queen. Even though she's got twenty years on me, not one of them show on her teenage-like face, her body as slim as ever, her pixie figure interrupted only by the roundness of her pregnant stomach.

"I'm sorry if my brother is being an ass," Adele chimes.

I open and close my mouth, debating whether or not to ask her about my engagement. She's queen, so matters of the sort should be run by her, but I know better than anyone how our fathers and husbands overlook our official ranks whenever it suits them.

"You're due soon, I heard?"

Her lips thin. "A few weeks at most."

I check the room, but no one is heading in our direction, and no one lurks on the outskirts of our conversation, so I lean in slightly and whisper, "Is it true? Am I leaving?"

Her forehead creases, but before long, the suspicious look on her face falls. "They told you, then."

"They did," I say, skirting the truth.

Her gaze flies to the ground for a split second. "For what it's worth, I'm sorry. I know he wasn't who you have wanted for yourself."

Tears mist my eyes. That's the understatement of the century.

"Duty takes us on unexpected paths." She motions flippantly to her golden crown, and to the ruby-red wedding ring shining on her finger. "I never thought I'd be queen consort, and yet, here I am."

"At least you're happy?" I let the end of the sentence dangle, throwing her a bone. If she takes offense, I can always pretend I was merely stating a fact.

Her jeweled hand twitches on her round stomach. "I'm about to be."

The ambivalent choice of word stokes my anxiety, and adrenaline pumps in my veins once more. "I need to talk to the king."

I scour the room and find Victor chatting with prime minister Chastain, both men laughing at some joke.

Adele grazes my elbow, stopping me. "Not tonight. If you have a shot at changing his mind, you should talk to him when he's alone." Her lips purse in a grimace, and she downs the flute I discarded earlier. "But I wouldn't count on it."

"Can you help me? Could you speak to him or your father? They must have conferred on the matter."

"I'm sorry, Ari. If my father and husband cared about my opinion, my life would be very different indeed." With a dry, almost bitter laugh, she waltzes off to her ladies in waiting.

Tears muddle my vision, and my undead heart aches in my chest. If even the queen isn't happy, my chances to find joy in this life, this court, are very slim indeed.

CHAPTER 14

EVERYTHING

LEO

A footman in full livery erupts in my room. "Mr. Callas. The princess has returned to her chambers."

The boy is young, barely out of puberty with a few rogue hairs on his chin, and his attire is straight out of a period novel, with white gloves and tails. Thank God I can wear whatever I want, as long as it's business casual. I'd die if they made me wear a penguin suit, let alone if I had to dress like a fucking English butler.

The intrusion spooks me, so I jump from the bed, discard my book on the nightstand, and throw a fresh t-shirt over my head. I thought I was off duty tonight. The coronation is a party reserved for the fang-bearing kind, so all the staff was pretty much looking forward to a quiet night until sunrise.

"Wasn't the party supposed to last all night?" I ask curtly.

He shakes his head. "She ran through the gardens like a bat out of hell, clutching the skirt of her dress. I figured I should tell you."

Heat blooms on his freckled cheeks, and I realize I'm being an ass to a human boy who was doing me a favor.

"Yes, of course. Thank you." I force a little warmth into my voice.

With a sharp incline of the head, he takes his leave.

Dread fills my chest, but I blow a deep breath out of my mouth to calm my nerves. She just drank from me. How much blood does she need?

Maybe she wants an early dinner, being a newborn vampire and all.

Sniffles echo through the boudoir as I inch open the door. The golden accents of the tapestries gleam in the moonlight, the electric blinds wide open.

"Oh, evening Leo," Arielle squeaks from the egg chair, the braided crown holding her hair up, half undone.

I nod in response.

She wipes the red tears from her cheeks and discards a fistful of tissues in the trash basket. "How are you?"

"Why are you crying?" My question comes out a little rougher than I intended, but my rudeness snaps her out of her sorrows better than warmth.

"Don't tell anyone I cried, please. I forgot myself for a moment."

"If you don't want to talk about it, that's fine."

I turn around to leave and walk a few steps before she whispers, "It's my brother. I learned tonight that he promised my hand in marriage to an old king I've never even met."

The cracks in her voice turn my legs to lead, and I curl my fists. "Without your consent?"

"It's politics."

"It's bullshit."

She drags her black nails over the fluffy pillow in her lap. "Total bullshit, right?"

I shake out the jitters, unnerved by this arranged marriage business. I might be sworn to serve her, but she's not her own person, either. She's higher on the pecking order, but we're both meant to follow orders. The realization mellows my anger, and I blink, taking in her appearance.

Embroidered roses embellish the skirt of her coronation dress, the intricate designs forming a tighter cluster over her breasts and stomach, the decorations sewn together over her shoulders to create two sheer straps that contrast with her ivory chest and neck. The gown flows to the floor, twice as big as she is, and her big blue eyes are still glistening with red tears as she pulls a series of pins out of her hair and unfastens the second half of her braid.

Her thick dark mane cascades around her face and highlights the roundness of her cheeks, her innocence...and youth.

Before she transformed into a vampire, she was a nineteen-year-old girl. A princess, sure, but I remember what it was like to be nineteen. I certainly didn't want to spend my time attending stuffy ceremonies just so I could be sold to some foreign king.

She's a demon meant to drain thousands in her lifetime, but I realize she's only ever drank from me, and my well-crafted armor cracks.

"Let's get you to bed," I offer, even though it means she'll feed on me.

She peels herself from the egg chair and heads to the walk-in closet. "Why is there a massage table in here?"

I can't help but roll my eyes. "I got a special class yesterday."

"Are you any good?" she asks in jest.

The change in her demeanor is so drastic, it makes me want to try and ease her sorrow, and I wave her over to the table. "I guess you're bound to find out."

"Wait. I need help with this first," she spins around and offers me her back. The corseted dress is laced tight, and I swallow hard. Dressing or *undressing* her doesn't strictly fall under my responsibilities.

"Can you manage? I can ring for help," she says.

I approach carefully. "I can draw plans for a canter-lever bridge, I should manage to unfasten a corset."

She waits patiently with her hands on her hips. "You were an engineer?"

"Yes."

Only...loosening up a corset isn't the same as undressing Arielle Delacroix.

Oblivious to my commands, my heart beats wildly in my chest as I gather her soft hair over one shoulder and tug on the threads of her corset. The cardboard-like padding scratches my fingers when I peel it away from her, the creamy expanse of skin underneath stealing my thoughts.

I turn around to offer her some privacy as she climbs onto the massage table, and the ruffle of fabric heats my cheeks.

"Should I keep my underwear on?"

My throat bobs. "As you wish."

Oh hell...

Why the fuck did I suggest this?

A snide, perverse side of me stirs to life. *You know why.*

"I'm ready."

She set a towel over her bare ass, but she didn't quite adjust it right, the roundness of her butt on full display.

Stop looking at her ass, she's too young for you.

Too young for me? She's a freaking vampire. Ten years is nothing...

A *professional* massage... I can do this.

I rub the oil between my hands, the friction heating it up, and bite my bottom lip. My hands shake as I spread it over her smooth skin. She's cool, but not cold. I trace the shape of her shoulder blades and unwind the tight muscles I find there.

An approving moan reaches my ears, the sound low and visceral.

Despite all my anguish, my dick has other ideas, and I'm infuriated by the desire coursing through my veins. It's not at all like it was yesterday during my practice run. I can't concentrate, and no matter how much I repeat to myself that I'm nothing but her slave, my body responds to her in ways I can't even fathom.

Remember, you're not going insane. Vampires are meant to attract their prey. It's normal.

Heat fills my gut, and my raging erection strains painfully in my dark jeans. All the inner pep talk in the world would not be enough to tame my desire, and my touch grows heavier, a little rough around the edges. She hums in approval.

The temptation to dip my hands below the towel or wander too close to her breasts is almost undeniable.

She's a virgin, and I know by now that the people responsible for her upbringing purposefully left her in the dark about sex. Until she marries, she's meant to remain a maiden, that much is clear. I'm the only variable in this scenario, since I'm a man and our relationship can't be policed by her brother.

Like Jean said, she can ask *anything* of me.

Right about now, I'd be inclined to give *everything* to her, but I can't.

Sleeping with her means giving up what's left of my soul. If I give in, there'll be nothing left of the man I used to be.

CHAPTER 15

TRIBUNAL

ARIELLE

T he night court throne room is painted in the blood of our
enemies, the blood of demons who broke the rules, and a
pint of human blood to sweeten the scent. Agony spices the
air, while the throne itself is understated, the chair cushioned with
black leather and a silver trim. The Delacroix sigil burns behind it,
the rose and cross drawn in flames across the wall.

Victor sits as our newly anointed king, and quite a few members
of the court are present to witness his first tribunal. All demons, Fae,
and other scraps of supernatural are bound to follow our laws. We're
the ones who make sure that no species or groups destroy the
balance or challenge the three Laws of Hatten.

The first law is obvious. If enough normals learned of our existence, our way of life would be in jeopardy, so humans and demons
who threaten to expose us are eliminated.

The second law states that no species shall reproduce beyond a
certain number, so that all kinds of demons can survive.

The third law is trickier. It states that no individual shall harness
enough power to be the sole leader of his people. That one is hard to

put into action because of all the secrecy surrounding the hierarchy of most demonic clans.

I sit in the box reserved for the highest ranking member of the court and peruse the program, curious. It's my first tribunal, and while I've read the transcripts of more than a hundred, it's exhilarating to finally attend one in person. Eleanor's name quickly glares back at me from the bottom part of the page.

Nomination renewal - Peter Chastain
Nomination renewal - Garrett Beaumont
Inquiry - The Louvre's Clay Gargoyle
Determination of guilt - Fiero Ranza
Tender call - Sweden hunting party

Closed audience
Reprieve of sentence - Sebastian Chastain
Special inquiry - Eleanor Delacroix
Determination of guilt - Eleanor Delacroix
Sentencing - Eleanor Delacroix

I bite my bottom lip. Is she here? Did they catch her and keep it a secret?

I wiggle on the bench, my stomach in knots. Elle was good to me when I was a bloodling, and while she killed my brother, I'm not sure I'm ready to see her head roll today. I crane my neck around, wondering if Lucas is going to show, and spot Adele standing in the back row, the queen holding her pregnant stomach. I offer her a small wave, but she's lost in thought, unaware of my presence.

I follow her gaze to the government official's box across the aisle. It holds a plethora of ministers with Peter out front, his amiable smile warming my ears. Behind him sit the three Beaumont brothers, my bodyguard off duty for the proceedings.

The court's warlocks ensure the security of the assembly, dressed in red robes with matching hoods, each of them standing in a separate corner of the room.

Many of the envoys and diplomats that traveled for the coronation are still here, so the gallery is full.

"Hey, Lil' Bit." Sebastian nudges my elbow and sits down next to me. "Excited to see my performance?"

His black satin suit gleams under the timid light of the chandeliers, his red hair slicked back in an attempt to make it look less red and wild than it actually is.

Back when we were kids, I would have plotted for days in advance to *accidentally* get a seat next to him in similar circumstances, just so we could gossip together.

But now, spooked by his sudden closeness, I jolt away. "What are you talking about?"

He taps his name in the program, encroaching on my personal space in ways that set my new body on edge, the several inches he has on me even more apparent than they were yesterday.

I pretend not to be affected by his proximity and roll my eyes. "How did you manage that?"

"Patience. You'll know soon enough."

I bite the insides of my cheeks, annoyed that he baited me into asking. My mother used to think that I'd need something from him one day. She even made it into a prophecy of sorts, her ability to glimpse at the future making her assumptions and opinions heavy with foreboding. But the only thing I need from Sebastian Chastain is for him to stay the fuck away from me.

"Welcome to the 11,253rd tribunal, his Grace Victor Turmund Delacroix presiding," the Maester announces.

Sebastian chuckles under his breath. "Turmund... your parents clearly didn't expect him to reign."

"Shh."

"Oh, come on now. This is just like old times." His breath leaves a trail of goosebump in its wake, and I miss the first few sentences uttered by the Maester.

The first two lines in the program are technicalities, renewing the nomination of Peter Chastain as prime minister and Garrett Beaumont as Master of War. The two men are dressed for the occasion, but Victor's announcement concludes quickly.

Sebastian leans closer as Garrett sits back between his brothers. "Our new master of war is quite handsome, isn't he?"

"Yes," I declare confidently. He's only trying to embarrass me, and there's no shame in admitting what the eyes can see—I'm not a teenager anymore. I concentrate on anything other than Sebastian's thigh touching my own.

"Only the youngest Beaumont got unlucky with his looks. That must sting."

Jasper does look different than his brothers. He's at least six or seven inches shorter than them, and with none of the mysteriously rugged charisma the other two possess. I try not to stare at Alec as the tribunal gets underway.

A clay gargoyle made the news in Paris for terrorizing a museum, and so it was swiftly put to death, a raucous poltergeist needs hunting in Sweden... My attention drifts back to the program.

"Did they find Eleanor?" I ask quietly to Sebastian, trying to mask the worry in my voice in favor of a regally curious edge.

Sebastian presses his lips together in a disapproving scowl. "That woman derailed the entire course of our lives. Why do you sound terrified that she'd stand trial here today?"

A hot shudder slices through me. "I remember how Ludovic treated us when I was a child. To him, I was nothing but a piece of jewelry he couldn't wait to sell to the highest bidder. Eleanor was a slave he paraded around to boost his own ego. If Ludovic's wife killed him, I'm sure he did something to deserve it."

He grows somber at that, the sly and mischievous attitude gone for a moment. "That's an understatement."

A nasty glare from the Maester silences us.

When we get to the closed audience section of the proceedings,

the gallery is emptied, and only the royal and government box atten-
dees are allowed to remain.

Sebastian sighs dramatically as he adjusts his tie. "Here it is. My
moment of glory. Take notes, Lil' Bit."

He steps out of the royal box and walks to the middle of the red
carpet.

The Maester squints at his arrival. "Sebastian Chastain, you're
here on a reprieve of sentence, and you have asked for a chance to
plead your case to the king."

"Yes, thank you for hearing my plea, your grace." With a slight
shift of his shoulders and a tremble of his lips, he no longer looks like
the smug, egotistic wildcard he is. No, like someone flipped a switch,
Sebastian now presents a perfect picture of atonement.

He falls to one knee in front of my brother. "I am here to ask for
your magnanimity, your highness. My wicked tongue led me astray,
and for that I was punished by your predecessor. My exile has
allowed me to see the errors of my ways, and I apologize, to the
crown and the entire court, for my untoward behavior."

I roll my eyes. No one present could ever fall for that, could they?
I guess it doesn't matter. Sebastian insulted Ludovic, and it pleases
everyone here but me to officially welcome him back to the fold.

Victor smirks at the falsely repentant vampire. "Get up, young
Chastain. I grant you your pardon, but if you insult the crown again,
I will have your tongue."

Sebastian bows his head in deference and whistles out of the
room by the main exit, but not before he throws a wink in my
direction.

I shift in my seat when Alec is called to speak on Eleanor's
escape. The royal guard faces the king, the Maester, and his own
brother Jasper Beaumont, the new head of the royal guard and his
direct superior.

His sunglasses are nowhere to be seen, and his uniform is freshly
pressed. The room goes quiet when he opens his mouth to explain
the circumstances that led to Ludovic's death.

I'm sure he's been questioned a thousand times, but the tribunal is meant to officialize any investigation findings and ensure transparency between the different branches of the government.

"The king ordered us all not to enter his apartments, so by the time I caught a glimpse of the alpha's scent, he was already out of the king's wing," Alec states calmly.

The Maester hikes his glasses up his nose. "Why would the king bar his guards from his rooms? It's highly unusual."

"He wanted privacy with his wife, Sir," Alec answers. The gloom on his face almost spells out what that privacy was for, and though he alluded to nothing with his carefully chosen words, every single person in the audience looks to the ground for a split second.

Jasper opens his mouth on a low hiss. "If an alpha killed our late king, we have to seek retribution on his whole clan."

Alec shakes his head. "No, it was Eleanor herself that killed him."

"How do you know?" his brother asks, his fists balled at his sides, clearly pissed to be contradicted.

A hint of a smile plays at the corner of my bodyguard's mouth, the change fleeting and incomplete, probably unnoticeable to anyone but the people on my side of the aisle.

She told me herself before she escaped.

I hold my breath, and a tremor of excitement runs up my spine. My nails sink into the wooden frame of the royal box, my knuckles white. I'm quite literally hanging onto Alec's next words.

He points casually at the corner of the room. "The warlocks have confirmed it."

The king squints at Alec. "You're mistaken. The warlocks couldn't come to a consensus about it."

One of the men wearing a red tunic clears his throat. "Actually, we did confirm it, your highness."

Victor shoots an icy glance to Jasper Beaumont. "Why wasn't it in the report?"

"It was a gross oversight, your grace. I'll figure out what happened," Jasper answers with an exaggerated, servile whine.

"Please do."

The Maester continues to question Alec, but my ears buzz, my hands still gripping the ledge of the royal box like I'm holding on for dear life.

Alec Beaumont is lying, and as he tells the story of how he was too late to stop Eleanor from escaping, I realize he let her go. Alec let Eleanor go, and the certainty of it settles in my bones.

He let her go, and I read his mind.

I have to talk to the king about my engagement and figure out who I can trust with that information. Quickly.

Two hours after the tribunal, Victor agrees to see me in his office, and the king's private chambers still bear the remnants of my psychotic dead brother. Ludovic loved two things: power and himself, and his portrait still hangs behind the desk. The painting shows him in a suit, his fist cramped around the skull of the Zhao King that murdered our mother. The sight dries up my mouth. They strike. We strike back. The endless cycle of revenge has cost both families many lives, and I'm the next in line to be sacrificed.

Victor dumps his quill into the ink pot and leans back on his modern desk chair. "Hey, Ari. What did you want to talk about so urgently?"

I force a cleansing breath down my lungs and close the door to his office behind me. I'm not sure how to break the news of Alec's betrayal and my new powers, so I bring up the unwanted engagement first.

"I heard about King Pereira. About the arranged marriage."

Victor fails to hide a cringe. "Damn. I wish I could have told you myself."

"Why didn't you? We talked yesterday."

My voice cracks at the end, but he dares to shrug in response.

"Don't get too emotional. I didn't want to overwhelm you."

Emotional?

Assaulting the king will only worsen my situation, and so I keep my hands firmly at my sides. "But he's old! He's at least 600 years old, and his reputation is that of a lowly, depraved brute—"

"We need Felipe Pereira on our side to defeat the Zhaos. It's as simple as that."

"We have the Pereiras. Lucas said—"

"Lucas is insignificant. The Pereiras do not go to war for their allies, but they'll go to war for family."

My jaw clenches. Not only is Victor interrupting me every chance he gets, but he clearly doesn't care for my opinion—or anything I have to say. He used to be so miserable under Ludovic's thumb. I can't believe he's doing this to me now.

"I'm a pawn in your strategy? A mare to be sold for her pedigree?" I try very hard not to raise my voice, not to appear *emotional* again.

He waves my concerns away. "You always knew you wouldn't marry for love. I married for power, and I'm perfectly happy."

"You got lucky with Adele, but it's an archaic way of thinking. Marriage is not the only solution."

He averts his gaze. "You should be happy. You'll be queen."

"I don't want to be queen. I just came home, just hired my staff—"

"You'll be respected. Lucas can stay with you there, and King Felipe will not live forever. Once he's dead, we'll rule half the world together." He picks up his quill again and straightens the stack of parchment in front of him, signaling the end of the discussion.

A cramp squeezes my ribcage as I stand. "He could last a hundred years."

"What's a hundred years to us?" Victor's pen flies across paper. "Look on the bright side, Felipe has had his children, and his legacy is secure. I'm pretty sure he'll let you go about your life as you please."

Pretty sure?

"The Pereiras are drowning in cocktails and designer drugs." I have no way to know these things besides the gossip I overheard growing up and the stories Lucas told me, but I believe every word.

Victor signs his name at the bottom of a few parchments, his quill flying about the paper. "If the court isn't up to your standards, then you'll change it. Little by little."

"So I'm to be a good girl and marry an old drunk?"

His gaze snaps up to meet mine, and he no longer looks distracted or withdrawn as he says, "A king."

The word echoes solemnly across the room. My brother heats a seal of wax over a candle and retreats into an uncomfortable silence.

I stare at him until he finally winces and looks up at me again. "You'll be a good *queen*, Ari. You're right, the Pereiras have been lax in upholding our sacred laws. I need you there to steer them right. They won't listen to a foreigner on how to rule their kingdom, but they'll listen to you. You're a Delacroix. Pereira might not be the prettiest husband, he might be drunk and lazy, but with you there, we can truly reform their court. Together." He rubs his face down with a worried frown, looking more tired than I've ever seen him. "If you don't, we have much worse to fear than war against the Zhaos. We could all lose our crowns, Ari. If we vampires can't manage to fulfill our duty to the Shadow World—if we can't uphold the laws of Hatten—other demons will rise up against us to take our place. I didn't want to burden you with this all at once—I was advised to ease you into it, but there it is. Much more than I need soldiers, I need eyes and ears in the Pereira court, and you're the perfect person for the job." He tilts his head to the side and laces his fingers in prayer. "Will you consider it? Please?"

Blinking away the tears, I lift my chin up. While I understand where he's coming from, and this is exactly the sort of task for which I've been raised—the sort of challenge that should be entrusted to my family—I still think the marriage part is most unpalatable.

"Thank you for your candor. I'll think on it, your grace." I take my leave with a respectful bow, pondering his well-made argument. The Pereiras do need to change their tune and work harder to uphold our laws, or the entire world will be in danger. Maybe I am the best person to fight for change, having a few ideas already on how to change our court, starting with arranged marriages.

Alec is waiting for me on the other side of the door, so I bite the insides of my cheeks hard not to show my emotions and hurry down the corridor, my new muscles primed for a run.

I should really embrace my enhanced physical abilities and test my stamina and speed. As a newborn vampire, maybe I could outrun my treacherous bodyguard and find a private place to cry without being judged or lied to. My fight-or-flight instincts are raw as I pick up the pace.

"Are you alright, princess?" he asks quietly, the now almost familiar question angering me further.

I spin around to face him, my chest heaving. For some reason, I couldn't bring up Alec's betrayal to Victor, but I'm not sure I can trust him anymore. Eleanor certainly didn't deserve what Ludovic did to her, but Alec lied to the whole court.

His gaze meets mine, both inquisitive and calm. I should double-back and tell Victor about his treason, and yet...

"Jesus, she looks so angry and disappointed. She deserves way better than Pereira. Arranged marriages should be outlawed," he thinks, oblivious to the fact that I can hear him. *"Why is she looking at me without saying anything? Why is she holding back? She must be in shock. I should really say something kind..."*

Taken aback by his train of thought, I tear my gaze away and clench my jaw.

Just as I'm about to head into the gardens, I collide with a solid chest. The scent of sweet peppers and cinnamon turns my head as Sebastian catches me in his arms, his proximity as confusing as ever.

"Slow down, Lil' Bit. What are you running away from?" He checks over my shoulder. "Beaumont is dull, sure, but he's not worth your tears."

Fuck. Of all the men I didn't want to cross paths with now, Sebastian was at the top of the list.

From the corner of my eyes, I catch Alec flipping him off. My bodyguard isn't allowed to show such cheek to Sebastian, but knowing both vampires, it doesn't surprise me in the least.

The redhead fiend squeezes my fingers. "I'm hosting a post-coronation party. You should come."

I tear my hand away. "Thank you, but no."

"There'll be plenty of young, willing humans for you to taste…" he adds, tempting the beast in me.

I'm already out for blood, so the last thing I need is to be surrounded by hot, sweaty humans. My gums itch at the mere thought of a drink.

Leo.

I need Leo.

CHAPTER 16

BUSTED

LEO

The evening after my ill-advised massage, I wake with a start at the sharp *beep* of my alarm, and the tent situation under my sheets sparks a fresh wave of self-loathing in my chest. *Ugh.* I haven't woken up in such a pathetic state since I was a teenager, and I cringe as I make the stupid choice not to take care of it then and there.

Instead, I pop a coffee pod in the machine and get dressed. Hazelnut fragrances waft through the air, making my mouth water in anticipation, and I transfer the hot coffee to a travel mug, about ready to start my day—or rather my night. I enter the princess' room quietly, hoping not to catch her in a bad mood or—god forbid—naked. The sight of the massage table is enough for me to growl, my erection still raging.

Surprise washes through me as I find Evangeline in Arielle's room, making the empty bed.

"Good evening," she says with a smile.

"Where's the princess?" I scratch the back of my neck, but a quick glance around the apartments confirms my hunch that she's gone.

"She left hours ago for the tribunal and asked us not to wake you. Are you ill?" Evangeline tucks the sheets and fluffs the pillows, her gaze darting from my coffee mug to my white t-shirt, and finally to my crotch.

My chest shrinks. "No, I—" I scratch the back of my neck, embarrassed. "Was Beaumont with her?"

Evangeline smooths down the duvet with a swift downward motion, a smile glazing her pink lips, her blond curls bouncing at the sudden movement. "Of course."

The stiffness in my spine eases. Alec Beaumont is different. When he moves, his edges blur slightly, like he forces himself to slow down to appear normal, and the jolt of fear I get in my gut whenever I look at him tells me he's the deadliest beast in the castle. He's serious about protecting the princess, but I wonder why she didn't wake me before she left for the tribunal. She must be getting hungry...

"I sent the new recruits to the laundry room, but I wanted to see you before I left," Evangeline says as she inches closer. "Can I help you unpack her things?"

I check the last piece of luggage on the dresser, only a few trinkets left for me to sort through. "No, it's alright. I'm almost done."

The handmaiden laughs, and next thing I know, her hand is cupping my erection. "Let me unpack this, then."

"Err—" I grab her hand right before it snakes inside my boxers.

She molds her body to mine, and I have to admit it's a great one, just not the one I want. "Come on. Don't worry about your princess, it's allowed, Leo." She kisses my neck with enthusiasm, the feel of her tongue eerie and yet not unpleasant, but I push her away a little more forcefully than before.

She arches a brow. "Are you gay? Because I can ask Quentin to join us."

"No!" My cheeks heat up under her questioning stare. I just sounded like I was disgusted by the idea of being gay, but I was incensed by the implication that the only reason I could reject her would be that I don't like women. Like there is no other reason that counts.

Like the fact that I'm fucking broken means nothing to these people.

She slips a hand below my shirt and caresses my stomach. "The first month is the hardest...let me help you feel better."

I shake my head. "It's all part of their plan."

"What is?" She finally stops trying to feel me up long enough to listen.

"They let us fuck so we forget who we are. We forget why we're here. We numb ourselves with empty pleasures like food, wine, and sex. It's how they own us."

She tilts her head to the side, her caresses growing bolder as she pulls down the zipper of her uniform, her bare breasts now on full display. "You're not making sense, Leo. Have you been taking your medicine?"

"You mean the drugs they feed us to make us happy? That medicine?" I snicker.

She drops to her knees and spreads my zipper open, and I don't stop her this time. Last night, my arousal almost had me do the unthinkable, and I don't know how I could have lived with myself if I'd crossed that line with Arielle. Maybe I just need to relieve some pressure.

I've been drowning for too long. A part of me wants this. A dry, wicked part.

Evangeline pulls my boxers down and tugs gently on my balls in turn, her other hand testing the feel of my length.

Her mouth is warm and wet... I brace myself against the wall at my back and let the lust wash through me, my boxers literally wet with pre-cum. I've been spending the last hours—even days—in a deep pool of sexual frustration, and this indulgence might be just the thing that I need to clear my head.

At least the cheery handmaiden doesn't own me. At least she's human.

She licks me up and down, and I can't resist the temptation to close my eyes and imagine the princess in her place. My dick throbs at the mental image of Arielle on her knees, in her damn corset, and my breaths quicken.

"Fuck, you've got the perfect cock."

I grip Evangeline's hair and thrust into her mouth. *No talking.*

Playing with fire, I imagine dark hair in my fist and a slightly fresher mouth, and my abs clench, the skin at the base of my cock so tight, I'm half-mad.

Until I gaze into Arielle's blue eyes, her ruby-red lips opened in a perfect "o."

CHAPTER 17
PARDON ME
ARIELLE

S lipping quietly inside my bedroom, I close the door behind me and press my forehead to the wood. It's not even midnight yet, and I'm exhausted. Heavy breaths resonate from the walk-in and tickle my ears, and I investigate the source of the sound. Evangeline is on her knees in front of Leo, her eyes closed as she sucks his...

I inch forward. The male anatomy in its aroused state was detailed in a romance novel my servant had sneaked into my bedroom at my request, but I've never seen one before. For better or worse, I no longer have to imagine what Leo's *cock* looks like, and judging by her smile, it's Evangeline's new favorite toy.

Trousers hang low around his thighs, and the noises he's making bring a hot flush to my cheeks. He looks enraptured by what the human woman is doing to him, his jaw slack and his hands buried in her blonde curls.

She bobs her head up and down, her cheeks sucked in, and gazes up at him with desire.

My tutors were always quick to skip over male reproductive

organs. It's fascinating how wrong I pictured how it looked, and I can't help but stare. It's big, for one thing.

Leo's shaft throbs. He moans before his green eyes snap open, his throat bobbing as he takes in the sight of me. "Fuck."

The handmaiden squeaks and scurries to her feet. "Your highness, I'm—"

I hold one hand in front of me in a halting motion. "Don't stop. I want to watch."

The words are steady enough, given that I'm bursting with jealousy and doubts. Leo can barely stand the sight of me. How is she so different from me? Maybe if I watch them, I can figure it out, and my beast is simply starving for it.

With her cheeks flushed and pink, Evangeline drops to her knees again, her breasts falling out of her unzipped uniform. A part of me wants to maim her neck and drink from her while Leo tests the feel of her supple flesh.

To my extreme surprise, Leo doesn't rebel. In fact, his hardened gaze roams over my body, and my skin prickles wherever his gaze lingers too long. My neck, my chest, my hips. I thought we were growing closer yesterday, when he massaged me with tenderness, but clearly, I was wrong. His eyes never leave mine as Evangeline sucks his cock, and he looks ready to *murder* me.

Blood rushes through his groin, the scent of it maddening, and my canines descend in my mouth, long and deadly.

"Fuck. I'm so close." A low grunt tears through Leo's throat, and his hips thrash a few times. Pleasure and rage mingle on his handsome face, and a hot line of jealousy burns through my belly.

Evangeline swallows his seed and licks her lips, her heart beating so fast, I can't think.

"Leave us," I dismiss her.

She runs off to the annex and closes the door behind her as Leo pulls up his pants, looking everywhere but at me, as I grip the skirt of my dress. "You prefer her to me. Why?"

"You're a vampire." He shrugs—fucking shrugs, like that explains everything.

My throat cramps to the point of being almost unusable. I didn't want it like this. I wanted us to be close. To be *friends*. "You can go back to bed. I won't feed on you tonight."

"As you wish, your highness." There's no false politeness in his voice now. He's pissed—shaking with rage.

I double back and find Alec in the corridor, a big ball of sorrow stuck in my throat. "Take me to Lord Chastain's party."

The feline bodyguard raises his brows, shifting his weight from side to side—the motion quite a big tell coming from him. "Are you sure, Lucky?"

I bite the insides of my cheeks hard not to mirror his uncertainty, my heart in knots. "It's not your place to ask, Mr. Beaumont."

If I'm to be sold to a foreign king, I should try to live a little. Use my freedom before it's ripped away from me. Besides, I can't trust anyone. Not Victor or Alec or Leo...

CHAPTER 18
WARM BUFFET
ARIELLE

lec is quick on my heels on our way to the two-story suite Sebastian Chastain commandeered in his father's wing. The space is filled with intoxicated humans, and a dozen vampires mingle with the crowd, but this is less of a *party*, and more of a *buffet*.

Some of the dancers already have bite marks on their necks. Alcohol, sweat, and perfume spice the air. The scent of so many humans in one place, their blood warmed by the booze and the dancing...it steals my breath.

My canines unsheathe instinctively, and I stagger, biting back a snarl, ready to jump at the closest warm body. The urge to pounce is so potent that I dig my nails into my palms hard enough to draw blood. Alec mumbles a series of curses as he steps forward by an inch, probably ready to tackle me down if the need arises, and my beast has got half a mind to test his abilities.

Parties like this are the norm for him and Sebastian, I'm sure, but it shocks me to say the least. No wonder most vampires here are males, a sea of young, pretty humans *ripe* for the taking.

Sebastian elbows his way to me, beaming. "You just couldn't stay away," he says with a wink. A form-fitting red jacket hugs his torso, and he's not wearing a shirt underneath, the smooth expanse of his chest only inches away.

I look down at my red dress and regret not taking the time to change. Judging by Sebastian and his guests, I should have worn something more...revealing, but I put on a brave face and answer, "I needed to get out of my room."

"Hey, Beaumont." Sebastian pats Alec's chest in greeting. "Sucks to be on the clock during the party of the year." Not waiting for his response, Sebastian wraps an arm around my shoulders and pulls me deeper inside the room.

Excited whispers and unabashed glances follow in our wake. A few heads bob over the crowd, women standing on the tip of their toes to catch a glimpse of us.

"Where did you find so many humans?" I ask.

"Humans crave what we offer, and the mortality rate at my *soirées* is among the lowest in the kingdom. With one word from me, they came in troves from the city and lurked in the village until sundown."

What a strange thing to boast about...leave it to Sebastian Chastain to pat himself on the back for only killing a guest once in a while.

The fact that the humans are willing to die for one party confounds me. They don't get any status, wealth, or power out of it. They will be thrown out in the streets by tomorrow morning and killed if they ever breathe a word of their experience to the wrong person. "Why do they come?"

"Because it feels better than sex."

Better than sex? I paw the skirt of my dress, my tongue parched and dry.

Sebastian's nose bumps the shell of my ear as he whispers, "You look hungry as fuck. Better drink up before you lose your shit. Do you prefer a dude or a dudette?"

I scowl at his language. My tutors would have scolded him for every single sentence. Hell, every single word.

Jason and Emilia preferred to uphold the decorum of our aristo-
cratic lineage, but Sebastian, Alec...even Leo seem to embrace the
new speech patterns. Maybe it's time for me to do the same, but I
focus back on the question.

"A woman." I don't know why, but I let my instincts guide me.
I'm angry with men today, and I better not draw more attention to
myself than necessary. My sheer presence here as a newborn
vampire and unmarried woman will raise quite a few eyebrows, I'm
sure. Maybe me feeding on a woman will not seem as scandalous.

Sebastian signals a tall, beautiful redhead woman to approach
and pecks her cheeks with a genuine smile. "This is my first-blood,
Fred. She's at your disposal."

My brows raise in surprise. "But we're not supposed to taste
another vampire's—"

"Ari... These rules are outdated," Sebastian chides, his lips
pursing like he's disappointed in me. "Fred is smitten with you, and
she's looking forward to it. I'm happy to share." He punctuates his
statement by squeezing my upper arm in reassurance.

Standing beside him, Fred stares, almost undressing me with her
eyes before she curtsies. "It's an honor to meet you, princess. You're
even more beautiful than Sebastian said, and my master is right—I
would *love* for you to taste me."

"Err—Thanks."

Master? Isn't that... a little too on the nose? I try to ignore the boom
in my heart at her praise.

She probably embellished the truth to be polite.

I'm not sure what kind of games the two of them are playing at,
but my beast is rising to the challenge, and I eye down Fred in a
predatory manner, giving her a bit of her own medicine.

Her black dress is tied behind her neck, two criss-cross strips of
fabric covering her breasts. A long, thick braid is tied neatly at the
back of her neck and falls to her waist. Cute freckles create
mesmerizing patterns on her neck, and I swallow hard, my mouth

suddenly filled with saliva and a bittersweet, entirely new zest of venom.

I'd been wondering how long it would take for my new glandular tissue to produce enough for me to taste it on my tongue, and I take its presence in my mouth as a good sign.

Sebastian snatches a flute from an offered tray and chugs it down. "Or someone else? Maybe you'd prefer a one-time guest?" He probably mistook my silence as a sign of refusal, but Fred's fresh, honeyed scent quakes my chest with hunger.

"No, I'm game." I lean closer to him, so that the music is loud enough to drown out our conversation. "How do you...make it pleasurable?"

He smiles wickedly, his jaw slightly opened like he can't believe his luck. "By Nyx, no one's taught you, yet?"

I hold his gaze, swallowing back my embarrassment. "Teach me."

It kills me to ask, but there's no one else I trust to hold nothing back. Sebastian might be a lot of things, but he's no shrinking violet. Another vampire would advise me against it, or try to postpone the lesson, but not him, and I need Leo to look at me without fear. This is the first step.

Sebastian's gaze darkens, his garnet eyes almost black as he licks his lips. "Oh—I will."

He grabs both my wrist and Fred's and whisks us to the roped-off section located behind the pillar of the mezzanine. Sebastian unhooks the two golden magnetic clasps barring access to the secluded nook and motions us ahead. Three velvet stools, a chair, and a modern loveseat are arranged around a low, rectangular glass table, the perfect spot to rest after a night of dancing. We're not completely out of view from the dance floor, but it's enough.

Alec melds himself to the shadows of the pillar, his hands held in front of him, his eyes hidden behind his damn sunglasses. The position allows him to watch both sides of the room, his body angled to the dance floor.

Sebastian motions for Fred to sit between us on the loveseat, the lack of armrest making it easy for the three of us to fit on the purple cushions. Static electricity sparks along my thighs at the friction, and the loud music pounds in my ears, the vibrations of the speakers buzzing through my blood as Fred unties the bow at the back of her neck to allow Sebastian more access.

The vampire angles his body to us and unsheathes his fangs. "First thing you want to do is grab their undivided attention with your eyes. Adrenaline washes through their veins when we stalk closer to them, but you want that first rush to mellow before you touch them." He cups Fred's cheek and gazes directly into her eyes. She shudders at his caress, and her pupils dilate until they're two giant black pools. Sebastian's voice dies down to a mere whisper. "Kisses on the neck help, but for that you have to exhibit extraordinary amounts of self-control, and you're not ready for that."

I growl at the jab, sliding closer to Fred.

Sebastian's eyes widen, and he shakes his head like I'm being unreasonably grumpy. "Don't scold, I'm a realist." He returns his attention to his prey, and I can't help but sniff her bare shoulder, the proximity of her smooth skin drawing me in. A small sigh parts my lips as I skim the shiny braid at her back, a golden, metallic ribbon entwined in her red hair.

"If kisses are too much to bear for now, use your fingers." He places two fingers on Fred's jugular. "Drum a slow, soothing pulse on their neck, about 60 beats per minute. Once their heartbeat settles down, use your tongue to spread your venom over the skin. It'll help make the bite painless."

Fred's eyes glaze over as Sebastian demonstrates his instructions.

"Fred is the perfect candidate. She was made for this." Beaming with pride, he leans forward and bites into her neck.

Fred opens her mouth on a high-pitched "Oh," the sound positively erotic.

Droplets of blood slip from Sebastian's mouth and trickle down the slope of her neck, and my teeth pierce my gums again.

I'm so hungry, and the beast rattles in its cage, the thought of tasting—and maybe killing—Sebastian's human woman sweeter still.

After a few meticulous gulps, Sebastian stops drinking and tucks his chin up in challenge. "Your turn."

My vision heightens, the music dulling to a faint rhythm, my senses focussed entirely on them. Her smooth, hot skin warms my hand as I caress the nape of her neck back and forth, using the motion to slow down her heartbeats. She wants this, and her abandon sweetens the deal.

The angle allows me more space, her leg still angled toward Sebastian, the untouched side of her neck beckoning. Her cheeks are rosy and warm, full of blood, and I lick a line from her shoulder to her ear.

Fred gasps and risks a glance in my direction, and the longing in her eyes is enough to send a thrill through my entire body. She offers me her neck again, and I kiss my way back down slowly. Partly to shut Sebastian up and make him eat his earlier claim that I couldn't handle it, but mostly to impress him.

I expect my childhood bully to chuckle or to crack a joke, but the vampire looks enthralled by the sight in front of him, and he licks his lips in anticipation. In all our years together, he's never looked more handsome or hungry. I drink in the intense curve of his brows and the sharp angle of his jaw, yearning to test the feel of his stubble and the strength of his shoulders, but my beast is tired of waiting.

It bites down on Fred's neck without an ounce of hesitation, and the warm human cries out, her back arching as she drops the halter straps of her dress. The two strips of black fabric fall at her waist, revealing her pert, supple breasts, and my grip on her upper arm tightens.

Sweet, sweet blood invades my mouth, dark, delicious and sparse, the mark of a well-placed veinous bite.

Sebastian teases the shell of my ear, his full, masculine lips slightly parted as he watches me feed from his first-blood.

I close my eyes and revel in her taste—a floral mix of honeydew and desire. The fear in Leo's blood always gives me a little rush of adrenaline, but this is different. It's insidious and delicious and humbling. I'm panting after a few seconds, my breaths heavy with lust.

I blink and meet Sebastian's hooded gaze, and he finally shifts in his seat. "If you pair it with sex, it's been said to be the headiest pleasure a mortal body can withstand."

A series of whimpers tear through Fred's throat as Sebastian squeezes her breasts, her nipples hard and dark.

The scent of her arousal fills the air, heady and strong, and I lap at the puncture wounds I just made. A rich and sugary flavor spreads across my tongue, each of her gasps spicing it up with a fresh ounce of ecstasy.

He teases her for a moment before he spreads her thighs and reaches down between her legs, hiking the hem of her dress to her waist. "Wait for the taste when she's at the crest of her climax. It'll change your life forever."

Fred is not wearing underwear, allowing him full access to her folds, and I can't help but watch as he starts to touch her there with the confidence of a lover who has done it many, many times before.

My own sex throbs as if I'm swallowing drop after drop of her impending orgasm, and I can almost feel Sebastian teasing her sensitive spot, her walls quivering around his fingers. It's slow and sensuous, Sebastian slowing down his movements to make the moment last.

"Don't stop," Fred begs.

She is writhing against his hand now, and I can't resist the urge to suck on her neck and pinch her pebbled nipple. A high-pitched gasp tears out of her throat before she quivers in our arms. "Yes, yes, yes!" she whispers softly, holding herself back from screaming like she might get punished for it later if she did.

Violent shivers rake through her body, and Sebastian holds her down so that she doesn't fall from the seat. "Good girl."

I shiver at the pulse of her blood in my mouth, and take a few extra gulps before letting go. My undead heart gives a hard thud as though it's alive again, and tingles buzz in my face, neck, and arms as I spot Alec there, the presence of the royal guard suddenly creeping back into my conscious mind.

I fight to catch my breath, my breasts so full and sensitive under my corset that dark spots dance in front of my eyes. "That was—"

Sebastian squeezes my neck and pulls my mouth to him, sealing his lesson with a quick, bloody kiss as Fred catches her breath, still sandwiched between us. His tongue tastes of her, and we withdraw before I can dwell too long on the bitter memories of our first kiss.

Fred staggers to the chair next to the loveseat in a daze, and Sebastian jumps to his feet. "Let's dance." He laces our fingers and wrenches me out of the shadows to the dance floor.

His proximity unnerves me more than before, the absence of a human body to unite us making this an entirely different affair, and I clear my throat, trying to appear unfazed. "Thank you for the tips, it'll make my life easier."

He presses his nose to mine almost tenderly. "Don't let them marry you off."

"I don't know how I could change Victor's mind."

He grips my waist with both hands, his touch rough and unrestrained. "You don't have to change his mind. Just kiss me."

I push him back with both palms flat over his chest. "Are you mad? In front of all these people? I'm engaged to be married."

It would be like a slap in Victor's face. It would destroy my chances to be accepted by his court. I can't.

"Kiss me and spend the night here." His voice is needy, almost brittle. "Pereira is old-school. He wants his wife to be a maiden. If rumors fly around court that you're not a virgin anymore, he might call off the marriage."

"I don't want to sleep with you, Sebastian," I breathe.

He chokes up, the sound almost savage. "Ah! Alec, then. Or your greek hunk. *Anyone* will do, as long as it's a very *public* fuck."

Alec is suddenly inches away, and he cleaves an arm between Sebastian and me to separate us. "Come with me, princess. Now."

Sebastian squeezes my sides harder, not letting go. "Relax, Beaumont. I'm just trying to—"

Before I can move, Alec wraps himself around me, the muscular planes of his chest caging me in. I wriggle to break free, but the acrid, metallic scent of vampire blood assaults my nose as a burgundy wave splatters my face and trickles down my neck.

A tall man with thick brows and a beard flashes into view. He's holding a crossbow, the tip of the bolt aimed directly at me.

"He's here to kill the princess! Seize him!" Alec shouts.

A string of gunshots pierce the air, the loud *pow, pow, pow* of his gun so loud in my new eardrums that I stagger. Shrieks and panic take hold of the crowd, dancers running for the door, the smell of fear thick in the air. The sum of it all short-circuits my rational brain to the point of helplessness, and if it weren't for Alec's soothing iron grip around my midriff, I'd rush into the fray like a fly that keeps banging itself into a clear window.

Sebastian bares his long, white teeth and dashes into action.

A silver bolt sticks out of Alec's shoulder, and a fresh one buries into his back as he whisks me away, his movements fast and slick. The royal guard plies me to his will, my head and arms tucked in, one arm supporting my weight and holding me to his chest. His body shields me from the projectiles as he heads for the servants' corridor.

"Where are we going? This isn't protocol," I ask, finally understanding what's happening.

"Fuck protocol."

CHAPTER 19
OUTSIDE PROTOCOL
ALEC

After we reach the servant's corridor, I tear the two bolts out of my shoulder with a grunt and dump them at our feet. The flesh itches as it starts to heal, but blood mars the princess' face and neck. One sniff reassures me that it's all mine, and I maneuver my charge deeper inside the maze of doors and narrow hallways.

Silk hugs the curves of her round breasts, her red dress simply sinful. The low-back cut finishes right above her ass, and my hands are pressed flush against her skin as I usher her along the corridor.

"Stop pushing, I'm going to trip."

I pick her up and throw her over my shoulder, the experiences of the last hour distracting as hell.

A tiny fist collides with my back. "Put me down!"

"You complained about the pushing. This is the alternative."

I can't believe Victor wants to sell her to a cruel drunk. King Felipe Pereira should help Victor in the war regardless, not blackmail him into treating his sister as a commodity. The old king has a sullied reputation, and old drunks with a perverted sense of self-importance shouldn't get to marry a woman like Arielle Delacroix.

127

Maybe it's not just about the war. She's young, fierce, and opinionated. *Sexual,* my beast adds with an approving growl. I know a bunch of men who are bothered by such qualities in a woman, especially since she ranks higher than them. Maybe Peter Chastain suggested getting rid of the princess to assert his control over Victor. Maybe her resemblance to her mother stirred up Victor's insecurities. Who the fuck knows at this point? The only thing for certain is that this second attack was an inside job. No one gets past the guards with a crossbow without someone looking the other way.

She raps her tiny fists on the small of my back, and I want to bite her head off for being so difficult, but my body has other ideas. One idea, to be exact.

"Will you stop?" In my efforts to calm her down, I end up with my hand flat on her nearly-bare ass. The hem of her dress rode up to her hips when I picked her up, and the lace of her underwear prickles the inside of my palm. The heady, sweet tang of arousal invades my senses, the shudder that runs through her as I grip the round flesh about enough to make me forget about the attack.

Oh Nyx, help me be strong.

She's not reacting to me, merely the sinful dance she was engaged in before the attack. But her scent... pomegranates and wine. All I can think about is how wet her underwear must be. I should rip it from her smooth skin and test the feel of her. First with my fingers, then my cock.

Gods, I'd love to make this snob of a princess scream.

Short pants rock her throat. "Is molesting your charge standard procedure?"

"Only when they're being difficult, Lucky," I say, but my steady voice doesn't fool me. I don't get a hard on for every royal I carry, let alone fantasize about wrapping their thighs around my waist and defiling them hard against a wall. The sharp pain in my shoulder only heightens my desire for her, adrenaline and a taste for violence lowering my inhibitions.

I'm not a trained assassin for nothing. My beast relishes the chase of prey and the art of the kill, and right now, it only has one target in mind.

I reposition my hand to her thigh only to realize that's not much better. I really shouldn't have picked her up at all.

Once the door to her chambers closes behind us, I lower her down to her feet. Her pliable body molds itself to mine on its way down, and I feel every inch of her curves.

"You shouldn't have—" she stops and flattens her palm to my chest.

Her left hip presses on the bulge in my pants, and there's no way she doesn't notice how aroused I am. Our chests rise and fall together, our breaths heated and shallow. I wait for her to push me away, but she just stares at her hand like it's a complicated math problem.

She's not into you. She's not into you. She's not into you.

Clearing my throat, I take a huge step back. "I had to get you to safety fast."

"Why are you so...hard? Are you secretly hot for me, Mr. Beaumont?" She arches a brow, a grin pulling at her lips like the idea is too funny.

I conjure a casual shrug out of thin air. "We're vampires. Blood and violence make us horny."

"Horny...yes," she repeats, eyes half-mast, probably high on the aftershock of human lust. "That's all it is then."

If I kissed her now, I would still taste Fred's orgasm on her tongue, and she would probably reciprocate, but it wouldn't mean anything. Everything that's happened is circumstantial, but a kiss would definitely get me fired. Or beheaded. One of the two.

The princess squares her shoulders, her breaths finally steady. "You can go. I'm safe now."

Will she report me? Ludovic wouldn't have batted an eye, but Victor is a wild card. In theory, she could have me demoted to toilet brushing duties just for the way I carried her in here.

"Hired assassins often work in pairs." I inspect the windows, lower the blinds, and lock the door leading to the annex.

"Then maybe you should stay." She arches a brow, and I'm not sure I'm in my right mind, but the way she breathes the words goes straight to my already stiff cock.

"You're safe," I repeat.

"Yes. Safe."

We're going in circles, probably both trying to remember that duty forbids us to act on our animal instincts. She hates me, and I'm not high-born enough for her, I know, but sometimes, those things don't matter. Sometimes, the only thing that matters is a soft pair of lips. The curve of a woman's waist. A pulsing cock...

Get out. Get out now.

"Stay here until I return." Flying out of the room, I concentrate on the task at hand.

Jude is already posted outside, and my loyal sidekick throws me an alarmed look. "I came as soon as I heard."

"I'll brief the king. Don't let her out of here, and no one but her first-blood should be allowed in there until I return." I rub my face down, not even trying to hide my turmoil—or my erection.

"You okay, man?" Jude asks with a hint of a smile.

I wasn't kidding when I said that violence makes vampires horny, the current circumstances offering me plausible deniability.

"Yeah," I croak.

He nods, and I hurry off toward the king's office. I trust Jude with my life. He's a true friend and my best underling. If someone at court wants the princess dead, I know I can trust him with her life, too.

BY THE TIME I ARRIVE, Jasper, Garret, and Peter Chastain are already inside, surrounding the king. If our late king Ludovic had one quality, it was his disregard for other peoples' opinion. Now that our new king is a push-over, the political cockroaches click closer and closer.

They stop talking as I enter, and Victor hurries over to me. "Beaumont. I trust my sister is safe?"

"She is, your highness," I salute my superiors with a stiff spine, crossing my fingers that they're not going to glance down at my crotch.

The king strokes his goatee and turns to Jasper. "Who let the demon in?"

"A blood slave admitted that she was approached by him to masquerade as a couple looking for a fun, bloody night," Jasper says, his ego bursting. "We secured the castle and escorted the visitors to the dungeons. Everyone but us and the royal guard has been confined to their rooms for now. We'll interrogate them one by one."

"Your son—" Garrett starts.

Peter cuts him off. "My son used the approved channels to provide for his blood slaves. Shouldn't we interview the castle's Bringer first? He's the one in charge of the human visitors."

Garrett's eyes dim the way they do when he's beyond annoyed but doesn't want anyone to know. "André is a loyal, devoted employee."

My ears perk up, and my brain starts to catch up with the events of the night and all the unanswered questions that carried over from the plane ride. "André Delamaison? That old crow is older than all of us combined, loyal to a fault, and he sure as hell didn't step out of line."

Victor pats my shoulder in a patronizing manner. "Alec... I think it'll be best if Jasper handles the investigation. I need you on a plane to Brazil in the morning. Bright and early."

"Brazil?" The word kills what was left of my erection.

Victor walks around his desk to sit in his chair. "Yes. Adele didn't appreciate her brother's stunt at the coronation, and rumors have it that the princess forgot herself in his presence tonight. She needs to join her fiancé as soon as possible."

I link my hands in front of me to keep myself from curling my fists. "All newborns lust for blood."

"It's not the blood that bugs me, it's her strong fascination for the pleasure bite. Her first-blood is a man, and we all know where that road leads. If rumors were to reach Pereira that she's not a maiden anymore, he might withdraw his proposal."

"That's bull—" I clear my throat, realizing my mistake as the king's gaze snaps up from his papers.

Victor wants the princess to exist on a different plane than us, a different time, even. The whole court holds her up to standards that should no longer exist, and they justify this travesty by calling it tradition.

Jasper stifles a giddy snicker with the back of his hand, and an awkward silence falls over the office.

"Excuse my brother's language, your grace." Garrett straightens his cufflinks, his Master of War uniform on full display. "He's still a bit hot from the attack. Aren't you, Alec?"

Bile rises to my mouth at how fake and servile he sounds, but I force myself to nod in agreement.

"A strong alliance with the Pereiras assures the princess' safety and the well-being of the kingdom. It's a win-win," Jasper adds in a blatant attempt to pacify the king even more. "Once the princess is married, she won't be in such danger anymore."

The way he said it...as though it's a known fact.

My forehead creases, a tingle of warning crawling along my spine. "You think that the Zhaos sent someone after her because they wanted to stop her marriage to Pereira?"

"It makes sense," the king says. "They don't want us to formalize our new military alliance."

Only...it doesn't. If this marriage was truly about a war alliance with the Pereiras, they would have kept it secret. Any formal plans would have been disguised as something else, and they would have made up a reason for the princess to visit Brazil.

But they did the opposite, spreading the news far and wide. Why?

Victor pats my back again, ever so condescending, and wrenches me out of my thoughts. "You're leaving for Brazil tomorrow. Do not let me down, Beaumont."

"Yes, my king."

What the fuck else can I do? This man owns me, and the day I openly rebel is the day I commit to a life on the run. I've tracked enough defectors over the years to know that's not a life worth living.

"Good. See you at the wedding," the king dismisses me, and I'm forced to leave the grown-up table with my metaphorical tail tucked between my legs.

Ever since I let the woman who murdered Ludovic get away—a woman I'd seen suffer unspeakable abuse—a part of me had shifted. I'm done being a puppet, and my hope for a new king, a better king, is quickly drying up.

I'm getting more and more fed up with the whole loyal soldier thing.

CHAPTER 20
BATH TIME BOUNDING
ARIELLE

Gurgles of water pervade the air as Leo fills up the tub to the brim. Lavender soap does little to cover Alec's scent, and I'm simply drowning in him. Dried blood covers most of my neck and chest. If I was still a bloodling, I'd probably be creeped out by it. Vampire's blood doesn't tickle my tongue with hunger, rather it's...intimate.

Only mates are supposed to taste each other's blood, let alone be drenched in it, flakes stuck to the nape of my neck, behind my ears, and along the curves of my breasts. The heated thoughts I read in his mind while he was carrying me are haunting, and I almost wish I would have found the words to convince him to stay.

"About earlier—I'm sorry," Leo whispers in the darkness, jolting me out of my daydream.

I'd been doing a great job of ignoring him, and my shoulders hitch. "Sorry for letting another woman touch you intimately, or sorry that I saw it?"

"Both." He swallows hard, and the way his wool sweater licks the bottom of his jugular is simply bewitching.

The shape of his shoulders, the sharp angle of his jaw...no

wonder Evangeline was so eager to drop to her knees in front of him. I wonder what he tastes like, down there, and if it's at all similar to the spicy taste of his blood.

An ember of jealousy flickers and dies in my chest. "I'm sorry, too."

"Who did this to you?" He's angry again—though not at me, for a change—as he unfastens the last hook of my corset and drops it to the floor.

I sink inside the hot bath water, the temperature divine against my cold skin. "There was a demon at the party, but Alec shielded me from him. It's his blood."

He squeezes the sponge and starts scrubbing off the blood from my neck.

I search his eyes, surprised by the gesture. Sure, he offered to draw me a bath, but I fully expected him to leave once it was done. "You don't have to do that."

"I want to."

I rest my head on the side of the tub and close my eyes. The rough pads of Leo's fingers graze my skin, and I surrender to his caress, indulging in this unprecedented act of pampering. He combs his long fingers through my dark mane and fastens it in a loose bun on top of my head.

"You must have been scared," he says.

"No... Maybe for a moment, but really, it's been a wild, confusing night."

Between Sebastian's kiss, the taste of Fred's orgasm, and Alec's wandering hands, I'm melting from the inside-out. Alec's leathery scent lingers in my nose as Leo washes me, and I grow breathless.

Adrenaline has been pumping through me all night. I'm a live wire—every brush of skin more potent and alluring than ever before. My nipples are hard and exposed, and I catch Leo staring at them.

"Fuck, they're perfect...so full and round. I bet she'd moan if I so much as brushed them with the tip of the sponge," he thinks, the ache between

my thighs becomes intolerable as I take in the loose, desperate thought.

Sex with any human would be fantastic. The heat and the blood mixing into sexual pleasure? That ought to be good. Sex with Leo...

My stomach squeezes with need. "Touch me. Please."

Leo knows how to touch a woman like Sebastian did to his first-blood. I bet he's good at it, too.

Lips curled in a pout, he nods, almost imperceptibly. The sponge scrapes my earlobe, down the slope of my neck and past my collar-bone to my breasts. The rugged, textured material chafes my nipples in turn, and I grip both edges of the bathtub.

Leo lets the sponge fall to the water and tests the weight of my breasts with his large hands. "You've never touched yourself before, have you?"

A tinge of embarrassment cramps my stomach. "I tried, but—"

"But?" he asks, breathless.

After I read that forbidden novel my handmaid sneaked into my room, I tried touching myself a few times to see how it worked. I never seemed to...get anywhere with it.

"I never managed to finish," I admit.

He glides his hand down my stomach and plunges between my thighs, below the foam, and my eyes widen when he rubs my sex. It feels...phenomenal. It's hot and wet and totally overwhelming. Arousal coats my folds, heavier and smoother than the water, and Leo glides his fingers along the sensitive flesh.

Water splashes as I struggle to find the right position, feeling like I could implode at any moment.

"Spread your legs wide. Keep them nice and relaxed for me, princess."

Biting my bottom lip, I follow his instructions.

By Nyx. It's too much. Not enough.

"I need—"

He sinks his finger all the way inside me, and I purr.

"Just trust me." He draws circles with his fingers, slowly, always hitting the same delicious spot over and over again. His brows are bent in concentration, his smooth, golden skin beckoning. I stare at the blood pumping along his neck, obsessed with the hint of a stubble visible below his chin.

I want to lick every inch of him.

I should save myself for marriage, but the need in my belly will not be denied. Leo is mine. No one would have to know, and even if they did, it's my business. Why does it matter anyway if I'm to marry an old king who doesn't even want heirs...

The thought of crossing that line with him sends me over the edge. I cry out in surprise as my hips buck, the sensations slick and new. Leo doesn't stop, but soon, the pleasure is too much to bear, and I jerk away from his talented hands, my whole body shaking. The clench between my legs subsides after a minute, and a smile spreads on my lips.

"Wow. That was the best apology ever. You're forgiven." I stifle a giggle with the back of my hand. Gods. My tutors definitely didn't cover this part well enough. They taught me to think sexual pleasure was an elusive feeling, but this is fireworks and chocolate rolled into one.

CHAPTER 21
DEAD INSIDE
LEO

Arielle blinks, her red lips curled into a mischievous smile, her breaths quick and uneven in the aftermath of her orgasm. When I saw her covered in blood earlier, it...shook me. I thought she'd been hurt, and the panic that came with that blurred the lines between my head and my heart.

The latter booms in my chest, loud enough to drown-out the wry, dry parts of me that are all about criticism and self-loathing. The snide voice in my head is silent for the first time since I stepped foot back on Hadria and slowly descended into this hell that is my new life.

Water sloshes around Arielle's perfect body as she shifts in the bathtub to face me, her soft, full breasts bouncing at the movement, her nipples pebbled and dark.

I wince at the pain in my groin, my pants too tight for me to breathe, and hold a towel to my crotch as I stand.

She raises a hand to stop my escape. "I want to see it. Your erection."

I freeze at the tight squeeze in my belly.

"Is that an order or a request?" I grunt, about ready to plunge into that bathwater myself.

She slides out of the tub, bubbles tumbling down her smooth skin. "I learned—I want to try something."

Water sloshes to the carpet as she prowls forward, and our gazes lock. The glide of her wet fingers tracing my jugular sparks a trail of goosebumps along my neck, her touch heavier somehow. Her blue eyes gleam in the night, flecks of silver and gold hidden within them.

Mesmerizing. Hypnotic.

Suddenly, it feels like my heart is being regulated by the fire in her eyes and the wind in her breath. Like if she was to turn away from me in that moment, it would simply stop beating, dead and useless.

Like it exists solely to please her.

My lids flutter, my limbs suddenly numb. "What are you doing?"

She presses her tongue behind her front teeth, and the corners of her mouth quirk up. "Relax, Leo."

Her teeth dive inside my flesh, and instead of a painful sting, my whole body throbs in pleasure the way I imagine a woman feels when her lover's cock enters her—when she's so wet she can't think.

"Don't—Oh, God."

Arielle draws back to observe me. "It's working, isn't it? It feels good?"

It's more than good. It's...deep and explosive.

My cock throbs, the intensity of it almost painful. If she were to get on her knees and suck me inside her mouth, I'd cum on the spot. She undoes my jeans with nervous hands before taking another sip from my jugular, standing on her tiptoes.

I growl, ready to beg for more as she palms me through my thin cotton boxers, my hips grinding against her small, perfect hand.

And I hate it. I hate how the pleasure slithers inside every single one of my cells and makes them vibrate to a whole new frequency. I hate how supple her waist feels and how hard I am.

I hate myself for wanting her, but I do. Every day, it gets worse, but this is Armageddon. How I am supposed to resist my deepest and darkest urges if she does *this*.

Shame sears my face, my breaths coming in sharp rasps, my fingers numb. I don't want to lose myself. If I fuck her now, I'll vanish, and there will be nothing left of Leo Callas but the slave.

I can't let that happen.

Even for a moment of bliss. Even for her.

I squeeze the nape of her neck hard—hard enough for the insidious pleasure to stop. "Make it hurt."

"Mmm?" She looks up at me, a crimson drop tucked at the corner of her mouth.

I cup her face with my hands, desperate to taste her lips, the empty shard in my soul screaming at me to kiss and fuck her until we're even, until I've used her body as roughly as she's used mine and made her scream in all the ways my heart screams when she's around.

I dip in for a damned, angry kiss, unable to deny myself any longer. My tongue slips inside her mouth, full of rage and grievances. The violence of the kiss betrays how much I've fallen for her and the hatred I feel toward what she stands for—what she is. She draws a sharp intake of breath before she melts in my arms, rising to the occasion and meeting every urgent lick and graze with her own, her hand still teasing me through my underwear.

I finally come up for air, more furious than I've ever been, feeling like the pleasure of her bite chopped away one more piece of me. "Damn it, Arielle!"

She brings a hand to her lips. "You kissed me."

"I shouldn't have. I was confused by your new... skills." I rip her off me, and she staggers backwards, her beautiful face twisted with the sting of rejection and the fire of anger as I rebutton my jeans.

And I run.

I run until I reach the interior courtyard. The sun is about to appear over the horizon, the sky streaked with high-flying clouds.

The cool spring air acts as a salve to my molten skin, and blood finally returns to my brain, my muscles burning.

Garrett Beaumont, the oldest of the three Beaumonts, according to Quentin, is sitting by the fountain with a tall, slender companion covered by a hood and cape. They both jump to their feet at my arrival, and I catch a glimpse of a bloody, feminine hand.

Maybe the vampire was having a quick snack before sunrise? His reaction seems to indicate that he was breaking the rules, somehow, so I let my gaze fall to the ground as his friend whistles out of view.

The vampire curls his fists. "What are you doing here? You were supposed to stay with the princess."

"I needed some air," I say harshly, unable to hide my current mood.

The vampire's eyes dim, but he doesn't reprimand me, or become aggressive. In fact, he calms down from his initial surprise. "Is she alright? The princess?"

"Yes."

He nods a few times, more to himself, I think, than to me.

After a few long seconds, he motions me forward. "Come, the head of the royal guard wanted to speak with you."

I look down at my clothes, peppered with the purple-tinted water from Arielle's bath. "Wait—why?"

I'm not in the right headspace to meet anyone, let alone the head of the royal fucking guard. In fact, I need a few minutes by myself to take care of my... problem.

Garrett straightens his uniform, the row of medals on his chest on full display. "He asked to meet the princess' first-blood. Since I have you here now, better get it out of the way."

I force a deep breath down my lungs and obey.

Garrett takes me to the guard's headquarters by the entrance of the estate, and we climb a flight of stairs into an alcove office that offers a wide view of the road leading to the castle and its surrounding area, with windows facing in all four directions. We might not be far from Marseilles and the Mediterranean Sea, but we're certainly equipped to hold a siege of some kind.

Empty bottles clutter the desk behind a short, broad vampire with an eclectic array of piercings.

"Callas...I think you're the first of your name to make it to court, Leo," he slurs, clearly inebriated.

I know he expects me to say that it's an honor, but I won't. Instead, I keep my eyes firmly planted on the ground.

The way he looks at me...it crawls under my skin, in a very, very bad way. Long dark hair is slicked back over his large head, and his perfectly straight white teeth seem too large for his tight mouth, making his smile appear forced—-or rather disingenuous.

"I'm Jasper Beaumont. I'm in charge of the Royal Guard and the security of their majesties."

I nod silently, my instincts screaming at me not to engage in any conversation with him, his vulture-vibe sparking a fresh rush of adrenaline in my veins. Alec is an assassin, but he exudes calm and professionalism, and Garrett is built like a brute, but sophisticated. This third Beaumont is all teeth and slime.

He links his hands in front of him, elbows propped on the table. "I've heard unsettling rumors about your relationship with our beloved princess. I don't know what others have told you, but she needs to remain a virgin until her wedding."

I swallow hard, a hard lump stuck in my throat, the wretched taste almost impossible to bear.

He slithers to his feet and prowls over to sit on the corner of his desk. "Do you understand what I'm saying?" The scent of alcohol thickens his breath.

"Y-yes," I croak, shaking inside from the urge to punch his face.

He leans in and cups my face without hesitation.

I slip from his grasp and raise both hands in front of me. "Stop!"

"Are you a stupid man?"

"I belong to the princess." I never thought I'd be so eager to say those words, but hell. "You can't drink my blood, it's forbidden." Maybe he's just drunk and needs to be reminded of the rules.

"True enough..." The click of his belt buckle is quickly followed by the sound of his zipper, and he grabs his already hard dick. "Get on your knees, Callas."

All the blood drains from my face, and my muscles coil. "No."

His lewd gaze snaps up to meet mine. "What did you say?"

Fate is punishing me for what I did, for being weak. I allowed myself one moment of weakness, one temptation, and this is how God punishes me.

I curl my fists. "I won't suck your cock, not now, not ever."

"A little homophobic, are you?"

"Oh no...I'm just not into drunk, arrogant bitches."

Egging the murderous vampire on for a swift death... I'll take that gamble. I should really thank him for the opportunity since I'm too much of a coward to do it myself.

He grabs my throat and squeezes it, hard enough to choke me. Dark spots dance in front of my eyes, and I squeeze the vampire's arm hard with no effect.

I'm human. He's not. It's not a fair fight.

A woman appears a the door, with pale skin, garnet-red eyes, and short black hair. A sparkling tiara decorates the short, boyish haircut. "Jasper. What do you think you're doing?"

The chokehold loosens a tiny bit as Jasper bows. "My queen."

"Leave the poor man alone and follow me."

The vampire releases me, but not before he squeezes my ass. "See you soon, Callas."

He leaves with the queen, and I escape his office with quick, hurried steps. Panting hard, I return to my room, aware I've nearly been killed—or raped. A deep bruise throbs on my neck, and shivers quake through me as I close the door of the annex behind me as quietly as possible.

This can't be the rest of my life, being ordered around and abused by every vampire with a pair of fangs. There must be a way to both save myself and protect my family.

If I was scared to grow soft on Arielle, I'm certainly not coming around to my destiny as a vampire slave. In fact, I'd sell my soul to see Jasper Beaumont burn.

CHAPTER 22
IDIOT
ARIELLE

"Who was he? The demon that attacked me?" I ask Victor as he paces my bedroom, looking over the trinkets on my dresser like he's gathering his thoughts.

Leo's been gone for about ten minutes, and the king surprised me with his visit as I was still pondering whether or not I should run after my first-blood. If he hadn't run off...our dalliance would have become really *public* indeed.

Victor picks up mother's jade pendant from the open jewelry box and twirls it in the air. "We don't know yet, but the longer you stay here, the more I fear you'll be in danger. The Zhaos have heard of our plans and want to prevent the alliance from taking shape. Have you thought on my offer, yet?" He sneaks a glance at me, trying to appear nonchalant.

I give him a solemn nod. "I did. Do you think Felipe Pereira will let me influence his court?"

My brother fails to mask a wince as he returns the pendant to the box. "No, I think he'll gorge himself on blood and sex until he dies, but that's not the issue. His lords and ladies will come to you for

145

guidance. I want you to befriend them until they trust you, and then we can bring them around to the reform that needs to take place."

A soft knock calls my attention to the door, and Victor opens it to Lucas, motioning him inside. "Lord Pereira will be with you every step of the way. You'll help your new queen win over your people, won't you, Lucas?" he asks cheerfully.

"Absolutely."

Victor wraps one arm around each of us. "Perfect! The both of you can work together on the inside, but it won't be easy. Vampires abhor change. Any splashy action will put them off, so you'll have to be smart about this. Take your time." Victor leans closer to my ear. "You'll have to rely on each other. Take care of each other. You understand?"

Lucas and me... the intense glint in Victor's eyes throws me for a loop, his words full of double-meaning. For the last ten years, I've repeated to myself, over and over again, that Lucas and I could never be together.

Now that I'm learning that the real world is not quite the romantic fairytale I'd hoped for, the fact that Victor is involving him in his plans no longer seems trivial. It's well known that seasoned kings and queens have plenty of mistresses and lovers... Maybe, despite what we've been told by the Elders, our friendship could eventually evolve into something more. Victor isn't sending me to a foreign court without an ally, and at the very least, I'll have a friend to confide in.

Someone has to try and get the Pereira court in order, and if the Zhaos are trying to kill me to prevent this alliance, it means it's even more important.

A shaky breath escapes my lungs. "Alright, I'll do it. It's my duty to our kingdom."

My brother cups my cheek, a wide smile glazing his lips. "Mother would be so proud of you." Then, his gaze falls to Lucas like he'd forgotten about his presence, and he clears his throat. "Thank you for your loyalty, sister. I wish you the best of luck."

WIND WHOOSHES DOWN THE RUNWAY, and the private jet's white hull contrasts with the deep blue sky. Lucas offers me his arm as we climb the stairs up to the plane, Alec quick and silent on our heels. The cabin crew is accompanied by another member of the royal guard, and Alec gives him a sharp nod as we board the plane. "Your highness, this is Jude Laslow. He's my most trusted man, and he'll be coming with us on our journey," Alec says.

I inspect the newcomer with a curious gaze. Since our first meeting, Alec Beaumont showed no true appreciation or loyalty toward any other living soul, not even his brothers. His manners are polite, but nothing more. Whoever this Jude is, he's a true friend.

"I thought you were a one man band, Mr. Beaumont."

"Every John needs a Paul."

"Who's John?" I say, pretending not to understand the reference.

Alec rolls his eyes. "Never mind."

His companion is built like him, and I offer him a meek smile. "Nice to meet you, Mr. Laslow. Or should I say, 'Hey, Jude'?" I wink at Alec.

Jude chuckles as he shakes my hand. "It's an honor, princess."

Alec shows Lucas and I to our seats in the first row, but I walk toward the back of the plane, where the staff is already sitting.

Bella greets me with a small wave, but I forget to smile back when I spot Leo, unnerved by his disheveled appearance. He's sitting as far from the others as possible, and my heart booms at the black and blue bruise on his neck. He covered it up with concealer, so it's probably invisible to the human eye, but the slightly darker tint of his skin is unmistakable.

"What happened to you?" I ask in one breath, feeling like I've been punched in the gut. "Who did this to you?" I raise an unsteady hand to the bruise.

Where did he run off to last night?

He doesn't answer, his face ashen, and stares out the porthole window as though it's an entirely different universe.

"Leo, please—"

He slices his head from side to side, his entire body shaking. "Not now. I *beg* you."

My mouth opens in shock, and tears well up in my wide eyes. Leo's bruise, attitude, and overall reaction to the pleasure bite are so jarring that I gawk, frozen into silence by his desperate plea.

Quentin slips out of the bathroom and bows politely to me, "Good morning, your highness." He murmurs a quick "Hi" to Leo before sitting next to him, but the tall blond man remains sullen and quiet.

Clearly, Leo is not ready to confide in me, and this is not the place to make a scene. We'll sort it out later, one-on-one, so I reluctantly walk away from him, doubling-back to my seat. But inside, I'm an inferno of hurt.

No one can touch my first-blood. No one. I'll find out whoever did this and have their head.

In the first row, Lucas stares at the ceiling with his head tilted as far back as he can manage, stiff as a stick, the weight and scope of our decade-long dream to change his court clearly getting to him.

I sit next to my friend, and his head lulls toward me like I'm his center of gravity. "I'm not sure about this. It's a lot," he whispers close to my ear, scattering goosebumps on my neck. "We'll have to find allies. People we can trust."

"Yes. We'll have to be real careful." I change the subject, my mind stuck on more pressing matters. "Quentin is a nice guy, right?"

I'm trying to figure out who hurt Leo and why he'd try to conceal it.

Lucas throws a glance behind us, probably wondering where my sudden interest in Quentin is coming from. "Quentin is the best. Since the first day, he's been acting like a puppy wagging its tail, ecstatic to have been rescued from the shelter."

"So he's not the type to brawl or throw a punch?"

Lucas' forehead creases deeply. "Never, why?"

"No reason."

My mind wanders back to last night, first trying to recall the exact moment Leo fled from my room, but a few other nuggets of the evening come into focus, distracting me from my goal.

Eyeing Lucas sideways, I bite my bottom lip. Another question plagues my mind. A somewhat inappropriate one. "Wouldn't you have preferred a woman to Quentin? I mean..." my cheeks heat up. I can't quite say the words, but judging from my body's reaction to Leo last night, having sex with our first-blood can't compare. It's a rush I bet every vampire craves to experience.

Lucas shakes his head like he doesn't follow. "No, why?" I give him a quick shrug, unwilling to betray my train of thought until his lips twist in a disgusted pout. "Did you really taste Sebastian's first-blood last night?"

His judgmental tone irks me, and I school my gaze to the front to erase him from my peripheral vision. "Yes. He allowed it."

"I thought we'd agreed never to let him manipulate us again."

"I didn't—" My jaw clenches, and I let the rest of the sentence die on my lips. "Sebastian might be a jerk, but he's the only one who treats me like an adult."

Lucas' heated breath tickles my ear. "Including *me*?"

"You knew about your uncle, and you didn't tell me. You *lied*," I whisper quickly.

"I was going to tell you."

"You had every opportunity, but you let *Sebastian* break the news instead. I expected more from you, Lucas." With that, I switch seats and sit across the aisle.

The rest of the plane ride is somber as hell, my gut in knots over my fight with Lucas and the terrible shade of Leo's bruise. In ten years, I don't remember being this upset with my best friend or more anxious about my life, and I sink my nails into my palms. The entire group seems to be holding its breath, and the TV screens, books, and hearts remain shut and silent for the entire duration of the voyage.

A sense of foreboding hangs thick in the air, like we're all heading toward our doom.

Alec finally slips out of the cockpit as we begin our descent. "We're landing in ten."

"Alright." I think back to the last time we landed a plane together and search his gaze behind his sunglasses.

Something passes between us. Not an understanding, exactly, but a weird current of energy, and a shiver quakes me from head to toe. The bodyguard's throat bobs as though he's about to add something, but he quickly retreats back inside the cockpit.

I head to the bathroom to change into the clothes I set aside for my first official meeting with my betrothed. The buzz of the air gliding along the airplane dulls as I shut the door behind me and switch the light on, the change in altitude pinching my eardrums.

The midnight-blue pantsuit and white blouse look plain and brittle under the fluorescent lights, and my fingers cramp as I button up the blouse. Anxiety crawls up my gut, the instinct to order the plane around slithering inside my cells. I work my arms through the jacket and fluff my long black hair over the collar, trying to hold the panic at bay.

Why is Leo hurt? Why didn't Lucas tell me about the engagement? Why am I going along with this charade? Why-why-why...

A knock jolts me back to reality, and I crack open the door. "What?"

Lucas pushes in and closes the door behind him. "About what you said earlier—" My friend grimaces, raking a hand through his brown curls. "I'm sorry I didn't tell you right away. I was...shocked to say the least."

Without giving myself time to chicken out or think it through, I press my mouth to his. His lips are soft, warmer than they were the last time. I feel as though I'm going to burst if I don't act, if I don't take back control. Sebastian's words about losing my virginity before marriage still haunt me, and I need Lucas to be on my side. Always.

Instead of deepening the kiss—or merely returning it—Lucas tears himself away. "Are you crazy? Someone could hear us."

My heart stumbles as I take in his panicked gaze. "You kissed me before my Nightfall."

"That was different. You weren't engaged to my uncle then."

"You always knew I'd be marrying *someone*." I frown, confused by his reaction. "We're both on the same page, right? I'm marrying Pereira just for show while you and I change things for the better at court. We could even...be together," I breathe, inching closer.

Lucas molds himself to the door like he wants to crawl out of here. "Think about what you're asking. It's treason. More than treason—it's wrong."

I push his chest. Hard. "Wrong? Are you kidding me? *Wrong*? Wrong is learning about my engagement after everybody else," I push him again. "Wrong is expecting me to be a perfect little saint while everybody else fucks around with blood slaves." Each sentence sends his back crashing into the door. "Wrong is trading our sacred laws and responsibilities for empty pleasures, like your court has done for *decades*."

I need him to retaliate, to show me that our friendship means something to him. That *I* mean something to him besides my title and destiny, but he suffers all my blows with a tired look, and I fail to get a rise out of him, so I stop. "That's all you have to say, then?"

"I don't know what to say. We're just friends."

"Just friends..." Feeling smaller than I've felt in years, I cover my face with my palms as Lucas returns to his seat. Tears threaten to spill over my cheeks, so I bite my tongue hard and make my way to the cockpit.

Alec is watching the pilot like a hawk, standing silently behind him as the runway becomes bigger and bigger.

The vampire is still wearing his big, opaque sunglasses, and I startle as he clears his throat. "We're about to land. You should sit down, princess." His polite tone is weirdly soft and subdued and so unlike him that it sets me on edge.

"You're not sitting down," I point out.

He grabs the metal handle above his head with a grin. "Then brace yourself, Lucky."

I grab onto the same handle with an air of defiance and raise my brows at him. Our hands brush, but I don't cower away, leaning into him for balance. I'm wearing high-heels, and so he holds me to him without hesitation, his hand both soft and hard at my waist. The pilot doesn't spare us a glance as he lands the plane, and before long, a fleet of black SUVs rolls in on the Brazilian tarmac.

Alec adjusts his cufflinks. "Are you ready?"

"Yes. Let's not draw this out."

The humid air assaults my senses as I step out of the jet, the scent of gasoline and warm asphalt colliding in my sensitive nose. I plug my nose with one hand and forge ahead, the numb tingles in my fingers back full-force.

Alec guides me to the car in the middle of the pack and opens the door for me. "Watch your step, Lucky."

The Pereira security team takes us all directly to a brightly-lit manor on top of a steep hill. The main building holds three floors with an open terrace on the roof. Hibiscus bushes flank the entrance on both sides, and modern floor-to-ceiling windows offer a wide view of the entrance hall, the Pereira clearly not as rigid about their privacy—or their aversion to sunlight—as we are.

The king stands at the forefront of a red carpet, and his vulture-like gaze hones in on me as soon as I step out of the car. I've glimpsed at a few pictures of him over the years, but none of them betrayed his age as much as his hunched posture does, and I grit my teeth.

Lucas' parents stand behind the king, along with other government officials in full uniforms.

Felipe Pereira grabs my offered hand and kisses it with his dry lips. "Welcome to your new home, Princess Arielle."

A cold shiver rocks me as I curtsy. "Thank you, your majesty."

The unobstructed view of the luscious hills steals my breath, my sight eager to latch onto anything but the gnarly man at my side.

"The death of your esteemed brother Ludovic was a tragedy," the king whispers. "You have my deepest sympathies."

He says *esteemed*, but he means *feared*. His silky voice is about the only thing that doesn't betray his age, but it's not pleasant, either. It's the voice of a man who's never been told *"no"*.

I observe the jaw-dropping scenery, sweat trickling down my back. "Thank you, your majesty. His death certainly changed all our lives."

I never thought my late brother had a redeeming quality, but he knew how to keep the other royal families in line. Leo was right, his death acted as a power vacuum, and this marriage proposal only came because Victor is considered by most to be a pushover.

I risk another glance at my fiancé and immediately regret it. His narrow eyes gleam wickedly, and his tongue darts out to touch his bottom lip like he plans to gobble me up. The elusive smile tugging at the corners of his mouth vanishes as Leo and Quentin come into view. The two humans are whispering instructions to the servants carrying our bags, and Felipe is overtaken by a fit of coughs. "Your first-blood is a man?"

My spine stiffens. "Yes."

"It is customary for us to choose same-sex servants," he croaks, his face pale.

"Delacroixs prefer to be more...open-minded."

He measures me up, his eyes flicking over me like I'm a dirty nickel he found on the street. "It's a good thing that you won't be a Delacroix for much longer."

Bile rises to my mouth. The old-fashioned custom of changing my name to match my husband's never even crossed my mind, my surname being the most revered one in the world. In France, women keep their maiden names, and I'd always assume I'd do the same.

"Rest now. You must be exhausted. I'll see you at sundown for our rehearsal dinner."

A nervous hiccup escapes me. "Rehearsal dinner?" We haven't even had an engagement party yet. Does he mean to say...

He straightens his tie, his gentle demeanor melting like sugar in the sun. "I'm not a patient man, little rose. We shall marry tomorrow night, during the blood moon, so our goddess Nyx can witness the union."

Alec's fingers twitch over his black jacket, the movement infinitely small, and yet so rare for the stealthy assassin. *"If he so much as touches her, I'll end him."*

I force myself to meet Felipe's gaze and try to convey my contempt for him. "We've only just met, your grace. Wouldn't it be smart to get to know each other, before we commit to each other forever?"

"Why delay the inevitable? I need a queen, and your brother needs an army."

The contract-nature of our arrangement is perfectly laid out here, and in a way, it makes everything simpler.

I crack a smile. "Why indeed. Please escort me to my rooms. I want to lay down."

Alec shadows my every step as a servant takes us to a secluded set of rooms on the other side of the estate. The mansion's tall white walls and floor-to-ceiling windows are covered with thin, modern electronic blinds to filter the sunshine. I could get used to the breath-taking view if I didn't already feel so desperate to leave.

Leo disappears with the king's staff, Felipe's men probably filling him in on the do's and dont's of the place.

Once we reach the guest wing, Jude stands outside by the door and Alec enters with me. The suite is bland and impersonal—no doubt temporary. Hunger tickles at the back of my throat as I consider the king-sized bed. A sense of dread claws its way up my stomach, the air conditioning too cold for my taste, sucking the warmth and humidity out of the room.

"Home sweet home," I mumble as I rub down my arms, hoping to erase my misery.

Alec inspects the bedroom, bathroom, and living room methodically, a bluetooth com tucked in his ear, and his feline grace sparks a flurry of goosebumps along my neck.

"Why do you keep your sunglasses on inside so much?" I ask, suddenly spooked—or rather-annoyed—by his *deadly-chic* look. "They make you look weird, not cool," I lie.

Adrenaline sings in my blood, and Alec is the perfect candidate to pick a fight with. Discrete, professional—and he already thinks I'm a nuisance.

He observes me with more interest than I expected, my jab apparently falling on deaf ears. "I have one flaw."

"Only one?" I muse.

"Yes. My eyes." He nods without a trace of humor and continues his search, pulling the mass market paintings from the walls to glance behind them and running his finger along the stacks of books as though searching for a secret mechanism. "They sometimes speak when I don't intend to. The sunglasses negate that problem."

"What are your eyes saying right now?" I ask.

He checks the windowsills and the lock of the sliding door leading to the balcony. "That you're as safe in here as you can be." He seems content with the safety of the guest wing, but the dark undertones of his voice set me on edge.

"That was weirdly phrased."

He pauses in front of the window, the moonlight caressing the edges of his toned body. "I think we understand each other."

Yes. I'm not worried about being attacked by an assassin. My soon-to-be husband on the other hand...

"You seemed annoyed with the king earlier," I say, fishing for the train of thought that led him to plot the king's death.

"I was. His tone wasn't appropriate."

I smile at his honesty. "Teach me to fight, Mr Beaumont."

His spine stiffens at the unexpected demand, and he turns around to face me. "You want to learn how to fight?"

"Nothing complicated. I want to know how to throw a good

punch and wrestle someone off—" One particular scenario comes to mind, and a shudder lances down my spine at the thought that my unwanted wedding will come with a *wedding night.*

A cloud hovers over Alec's features, his eyes still hidden behind dark mirrors and reflecting only my own anger. "Protecting you is *my* job, princess."

"I'm a vampire now." A dry chuckle escapes him as he rubs down his face, and I lift my chin. "Am I not strong enough to defend myself?"

Just as my heart is about to harden into stone, he removes his sunglasses. "Oh, you're strong enough."

"Then what's the problem?"

The weight of his gaze almost floors me as he prowls closer, his movements so slick he doesn't even stir the pieces of lint floating in the air. "He's an idiot."

For an instant, I wonder if he spoke the words out loud. "Pardon me?"

His fresh breath flutters down the slope of my neck. "Lord Pereira. He's an idiot. He should have kissed you back. You were right. About everything."

My throat bobs. I should scold him for speaking of Lucas in such terms, but I'm too stunned to speak. And I agree. One hundred percent.

His heated gaze flicks to my lips. While I feel utterly humiliated, knowing that Alec heard everything that transpired in the bathroom of the plane, the clear meaning of his words and the golden gleam in his garnet eyes tie up my tongue.

"You think I'm a *snob princess.*"

"I never said that."

"You thought it, though."

"Maybe." A smile tugs on the corners of his mouth as he cups the side of my face. He clearly doesn't think I meant it as a fact, his mood unchanged by my veiled admission that I read his thoughts.

We both freeze, suspended in this moment. Alec's hand trembles over my cheek, and in the small twitch of his fingers, I feel every bit of his restraint.

He squints at me. "Will you fire me if I kiss you?"

"Try and find out."

Ever since I was drenched in his blood, his scent—leather and honey—does twisted things to my brain. I want to bathe in his blood again and drag his skin across mine. My tongue darts outs to wet my lips, and before I can find out exactly how good of a kisser my infuriating bodyguard is, the door is yanked open behind me.

In the blink of an eye, Alec is back to his original position by the window, his posture as professional as ever.

"Is everything all right with your room, your highness? Do you want me to help you change?" A handmaiden asks too politely, her intrusion as calculated as her gaze.

"Yes. I'm ready." I clear my throat loudly. "Thank you, Mr. Beaumont. That'll be all."

Alec hikes his sunglasses up his nose and slithers out, and I'm left in shambles without him, struggling to catch my breath. One second later, and we would have been caught red-handed. One second later, and my future here, along with my reputation and overall chances to fulfill my duty to my family, would have been shot to hell.

CHAPTER 23
WASTE AWAY
ARIELLE

The dark spectacle of the Pereiras' court almost blinds me as I walk down the length of the ballroom's mezzanine. One story below, jugglers throw around lit torches while acrobats spin above the guests' heads in artful and seductive poses. Intricate delicacies are being passed around by human waiters dressed like they belong on a haute-couture runway. Huge glass panes have been removed to connect the ballroom with the open-air terrace on the roof, the weather still hot and humid.

The king presides over the party from his throne at the bottom of the stairs, a trio of human girls sitting on the floor next to him.

Multi-colored gowns sway in all directions to a hypnotic beat that makes the floor vibrate under my heels. Sequins, silk, chiffon and satin brush the checkered marble floors as red cups are being served, wine and blood flowing like a never-ending crimson river.

The train of my dress drags along the marble as I approach the sumptuous staircase overlooking the party. Orchid garlands snake around the banister, their pink, purple and white petals bent to the florist's will—as all ornaments are meant to be.

The king clearly expects me to be one of them, and I swallow hard, the edge of my feet teetering over the top step.

"We're far from home now, aren't we, Mr. Beaumont?" I say.

Alec's shoulders hitch. Though he shadows my every step, I never speak to him in such instances, expected to pretend that he doesn't exist, but I'm acutely aware of his presence as he nips at my heels. In the beginning, I felt like a prey he was pursuing, but now...now I think of the gleam in his eyes when he leaned down to kiss me.

He presses his lips together and offers a curt nod in response. "Indeed."

It would be easy to be swept away by the current and drown in the glittering dazzle of this court. I could dance the night away, toasting to the king's health. He means to use my beauty as a symbol of his reign, envied by all for his young, blue-blooded wife. I bet most of his lords and ladies will spy on me until dawn, hoping to glimpse at a weakness or a flaw.

They call this a rehearsal dinner, but I suspect any reason to party is a good reason in their books.

In reality, the opulence barely veils their barbarism. The waiters are blood slaves, and the girls on the king's arms painted their mouths red and sprinkled glitter in their hair to hide how badly their knees are shaking.

Felipe's lewd gaze brings chills to my neck, and I grip the railing. "Don't leave me alone tonight, not even for a second."

Alec steps closer ever so slightly, the heat of his hand delicious on my lower back. "At your command, princess."

The quietness of his voice and his lack of cheekiness shivers through my entire body as the loud music dies down.

"Princess Arielle Delacroix," the butler announces.

The lords and ladies raise their glasses in cheer and offer me a quick bow. Sweat, jealousy, and servility fill the air—as long as we serve them fine wines and quench their thirst for blood and entertainment, we own them. The drums awaken my cold heart, and the fury in my veins pumps harder for every guitar string pulled.

I've studied this. I've been warned against the temptations that come with my new body and the insidious ways they can be used to manipulate me.

The rich pulse of an opened vein.

The dizzying effect of music on our enhanced ears.

The debauchery of flesh brushing flesh, the need to be touched the most treacherous need of all.

I've been raised to believe that I am above all the tricks that royals use to retain power. We offer our subjects the very distractions that make them weak and easier to control. I've only ever heard about the particular tastes of the Pereira clan in lewd rumors, and I couldn't quite believe it until this moment. The delicious perfume of old wine and fresh blood clogs the air, and I hear the humming in my bones. I understand why those distractions are so appealing. Who'd choose politics and duty over this dance of the senses, this tailored offering of everything my body longs for?

Warmth. Sex. Oblivion.

To feel so much that you feel nothing.

My heart thuds along sluggishly as I greet my host and soon-to-be husband. No matter how often I repeat the words in my head, they still sound wrong and distorted.

King Felipe stands and raises his big golden cup as I draw near. "Come, my sweet, and admire your kingdom."

A bit of wine spills to the floor and splashes on my velvet slippers.

"It's beautiful," I say politely, knowing no good can come out of antagonizing an inebriated king.

"Ah. I know that look. You'll get used to the noise. You'll even learn to love it. Your court is still denying the essence of what we are."

"And what are we?"

"Better." His crooked smile is all teeth and thorns. "Here's a gift for you, my sweet."

A servant hands him a square box. He opens it for me, plucks the necklace from its velvet bed, and quickly snakes it around my throat. "A token to mark our engagement. I want you to wear it for our wedding tomorrow."

The heavy metal snares around my neck, the crude links of the necklace reminiscent of a chain.

"It's...unique," I say, unable to conjure the word *beautiful* for such a bizarre piece of jewelry.

"Everything that matters is. That's what separates us from everyone else. The power we yield makes us the most unique of our kin, my sweet, and that sets us apart, forever."

The wide-eyed women sitting at the base of his throne already have bite marks on their necks, and beads of sweat shine on their foreheads. Sebastian's party had similar tones, but it doesn't compare. I suppose that, in some ways, we are the same, but we're being more subtle about it. Maybe it's better to have our lust for blood, sex, and violence in the open. Maybe that's the point.

Just as I'm about to find some wisdom in Felipe's words, he adds, "I'm not sure I can wait until tomorrow."

"You'll have to," I answer quickly, but Felipe's slimy hand reaches down to the soft flesh of my ass.

Before I can move, Alec immobilizes the king's wrist in mid-air. "Hands off, or I will tear out your arm."

His deadly calm tone shivers through me, and I glance at the dancers, wondering if anyone is watching. The last thing I need is for Alec to be arrested.

"Are you stupid, boy?" Felipe snickers in disbelief.

"Hands. Off."

"I'm King."

"You're no king of mine, and my princess has respectfully asked you to *wait*," Alec repeats patiently, the way you speak to a spoiled, rowdy child.

I sidestep away from Felipe and try to defuse the situation. "You can wait another day, surely? I'm sure these women will gladly take care of you."

"Ah yes, they will. Tomorrow, then." The wickedness of his smile tells me I'll pay for this, one way or another. *Look at that tight ass, I bet she'll bleed when I enter her.*

The aftertaste of the king's crude thought turns my blood to ice, and I take advantage of a new Lord's arrival to sneak away. Shaking from head to toe, I elbow my way through the dancers, Alec quick on my heels.

I snatch a wine glass from a tray and empty it in one swig, the alcohol warming my chest slightly. It sickens me that this drunk, misogynistic old pig will get to rule over my body, but I will not give him my heart. Nor my wits.

"Do you think I can change these people, Mr Beaumont? Do you believe that, with time, I could convince them to drink less and work more?" I ask, suddenly feeling like it's quite an impossible task.

"I doubt it, your grace."

I nod in agreement, my stomach in knots. Whether Victor embellished his views of my position here on purpose or not, I will not let my spirit be broken by this cruel, cruel hand fate has dealt me.

I will be queen.

I will find a way to make this work for me and change things for the better.

I have to.

... Oh Gods...

What if I can't?

The thought brings a bitter tang to my mouth, and I realize I've nicked my tongue with my new pair of sharp canines. Alec looms behind me, but I don't dare to look at his face, terrified of the emotions it might stir up.

I make my way to Lucas instead, desperate for a friendly ear. "Can you believe this?"

The young vampire stares down at the bottom of his own cup, hidden in the back of the crowded room. "Mm?"

"It's much worse than we heard. Did you know? I'm not sure we'll be able to do much, not if everyone here is drugged." I snort at the ridiculousness of it all. "It's hard to think any of these lords can sober up long enough to hear our pleas, fight in any war, or hunt outlawed demons efficiently. They can barely stand up."

His shoulders move uncomfortably underneath his jacket, his gaze avoiding mine at all cost. "They're not so bad."

Right. Most of the men here are related to him in some way. He rejected me in the plane, and that stings, but the crafted, completely fake aloofness he exudes now stings harder.

Lucas pushes himself off the wall. "We can't constantly be seen together. It'll look suspicious."

And with that, my childhood friend walks away, tearing up all the memories we made together.

As I swallow back fresh tears, a discreet, gentle graze ghosts along my back, and I shudder at the implications.

Alec Beaumont might get on my nerves, he might be the most insufferable, arrogant bodyguard the world has ever known, but he's my only true ally here. Leo hates me, and Lucas made his allegiance clear.

I chat with a few lords and ladies, exchanging pleasantries for the better part of the night while the king gorges himself on his blood slave, oblivious to my presence.

Feeling desperate and numb, I search the room for an escape and collide with a striking, powdery-blue gaze. My mouth opens in surprise, and I excuse myself from the empty conversations before inching toward the back of the room.

The blue-eyed stranger is leaning on the bar. A velvet-blue suit highlights his broad shoulders, chestnut curls lick the top of his brows, and a crafted air of innocence clings to his boyish face. A bright halo of power shimmers around his head, and the air catches in my throat, the sight of the immortal sparking a flare of longing in my belly.

The man blinks over to me—by the bar one moment and besides me the next. He bows, eyes cast down. "I'm Keenan McCaillin. At your service, princess." A thick accent laces his words—low and ancient.

"You're an angel."

"In the flesh. I've been tasked with your welfare by the king."

I raise my wine glass to Alec standing barely a foot behind me. "Get in line. I already have a bodyguard."

"Yes, well, your friend here is expected to return home after the wedding. I'm here to replace him when he leaves."

My eyes bounce to Alec, and his gaze drops to the floor, confirming the stranger's claim. My chest contracts, tight and painful.

When Alec leaves, I will be utterly and completely alone.

Working hard to seem unaffected, I skim the lapels of the angel's smooth jacket. "I'm surprised the king would choose you to watch over me."

"If you mean that he's an intensely jealous creep—and that I'm a hunk—thank you."

I mask a laugh with my hand, delighted by his answer. "McCaillin...are you Irish?"

"Celt."

I squint at him and concentrate on his blue gaze, trying to read his thoughts, but the more I try, the more peaceful and calm I feel until I almost forget to breathe. I shake off his thrall and switch gears.

"How does an ancient, powerful angel end up serving a vampire king halfway across the world? Was our court not to your liking?" I ask.

He brings a hand to his chest. "Ancient. Ouch. But you're right, it's a wee bit unorthodox."

"Angels are only males, right?"

"Aye."

If I wasn't so on edge, I might daydream about an entire species of Celtic, muscular men who also feed on humans while maintaining their warm blood and hot bodies...but this one is working for the king that bought me from my brother, so I doubt he'd be sensitive to my position as the mail-order bride.

"What's the catch? Why did the king really hire you?" The man who scolded me about Leo wouldn't hire someone even more attractive and sexual to shadow my every step. No, something weird is going on.

The angel tilts his head to the side. "You were attacked back in Europe. It's not a stretch to imagine your enemies would do anything to stop the wedding."

"But that's not really why you're here."

His gaze bounces to the throne for a moment, and he swipes his thumb across his bottom lip. "You're not at all how I pictured you to be."

"Is that a compliment?"

"Yes. I'll see you soon, princess." The man blinks out of the room, there one second and gone the next.

I cower closer to Alec. "Mr. Beaumont, can you enlighten me? What the hell is going on here?"

My bodyguard stiffens. "Keenan is more into my line of work."

"An assassin?"

"Yes."

"You mean he's here—for me?"

A wolfish smile blooms on his lips. "Oh no, Lucky. If Keenan was here to kill you, he'd already be dead."

"Who then?"

He searches the room, his piercing gaze sexy as hell. "That's what I have to find out."

My gaze flicks over to him, my heart in pieces. "Before you leave, you mean?"

"Yes." Alec grips my arm, gentle but firm. "This way, princess."

Tingles spread across my skin at the unexpected touch. "Where are we going?"

"It's a shortcut to your room. I figured you might want to retire early, given the circumstances." He glances at me sideways as I follow him.

Something's off with him, too.

When we reach my door, I expect him to mention our aborted kiss—or at the very least dive in for another try—but adrenaline rushes in my blood at the dark, closed expression on his face. I choke on a snicker of disappointment when he slides away from me in a smooth—but undoubtedly deliberate—way. I search his gaze for a clue.

"What a stupid thing to do...he'll punish her for it, because of me..." he thinks, the mental speech laced with agony. *"I had to get her here in one piece, but now...I've made things much worse."*

Of course, Alec Beaumont is merely fulfilling his mission. When this is all over, he'll return to France for his next orders. He's no doubt eager to return to his assassin ways. Despair settles in my bones, my tongue parched and dry. I've drank too much wine and not enough blood. I'm holding in too much sorrow.

"When are you leaving?" I enunciate the words slowly, trying to regain my composure.

"A couple of days after the wedding—at most."

I nod in understanding, my throat tight and painful. He was here to see his princess safely to her destiny, but his talents will not be wasted with the likes of a foreign queen. Starting tomorrow, that's all I'll ever be. I'll stop being a Delacroix as soon as the Elder confirms the union. Arielle Pereira will waste away in a court of thorns and ruin, and no one will mourn her.

"Goodnight, Mr. Beaumont," I breathe as I slip inside the confines of my room.

Just thinking about the way he pressed his hand on the small of my back earlier dizzies me, and a tiny voice in my head whispers for me to say something more, to beg him to stay, but I resist the urge to make a fool of myself. If he's leaving, then that's that. I can't afford to add a broken heart to my list of problems.

CHAPTER 24

DUTY

ARIELLE

The door shuts behind me with a soft *thud*, and I walk to the back of the room, unfastening the heavy necklace Felipe gave me. Leo stands up from the decorative chair in the corner, the Pereira-appointed chaperone at his side, and the beast inside me screams to be let out, my thirst for him only heightened by all the emotions running wild between us.

I muffle a quiet sob with my hand as I hand him the necklace. "Good evening, Leo." I turn to his companion, trying to convey exactly how much his presence irks me. "I've decided to retire early, and I'm hungry. Would you be so kind as to take this to Bella, my seamstress, and ask her to adjust the wedding dress' neckline to fit with this...*thing*."

I know he's here to spy on Leo and I, but he can't oppose such a direct order, so he takes the necklace from me. "Immediately, your grace."

I sit on the chaise lounge to pry off my heels as he leaves. Leo's tall, muscular frame hovers above me, so I risk a glance in his direction. A white t-shirt sticks to his skin, the humid air of this new continent lacing his usual scent with hints of night jasmine, liquor, and sunshine. The squeeze in my gut almost compels me to bite him, the need to touch him almost imperious.

Air whistles out of his mouth, his face ashen. "I know this wedding isn't what you want."

I place my hands flat on my thighs. "It's my duty."

His eyes soften, and he looks at me straight in the eyes for the first time since the bathtub incident. "I understand."

"You mean because you did the same?" I stand, our bodies barely a hair's-width apart, the few inches he has on me so noticeable in the dim light. I search his face for the truth. "Tell me. I'm tired of you walking on eggshells. Tell me being my first-blood wasn't what you wanted."

He licks his lips, looking everywhere but at me. "Alright, it wasn't what I wanted."

My jaw ticks at the pain in his voice, but I force a deep breath down my lungs and try to keep my voice from sounding too reproachful as I ask, "Then why did you come to the choosing ceremony?"

He pauses for an entire minute, but I patiently await his response. Some words are simply harder to find than others. "My mother was sick. Our family's candidate had just died in an accident, so the Bringer promised a magical cure for my mother in exchange for my presence at the ceremony."

The sweet tremble of his voice melts my heart, and my chest heaves, his honesty poignant and raw. I don't mention the fact that, with one word from him, one inkling of how he truly felt, all of this could have been avoided. It wouldn't be kind to mention it, and—truth be told—I'm still glad I chose him. "And you hate me for choosing you."

His gaze darts to the ground, almost as heart-wrenching and elusive as his quick, "Yes."

My throat constricts to the point of being almost unusable. "And now?"

"I don't hate you, princess."

PRINCESS OF THORNS AND RUIN

The admission allows for a tiny flicker of hope, and a sad smile tugs at my lips. "That's a start. Maybe from now on, we could be more honest with each other?"

He smiles back, the sight almost divine. "I think that's a good idea."

I motion for him to sit on the nearby chair and open my mouth to ask about his bruise but decide against it, his earlier reaction still fresh in my mind. He seems to be opening up, and I don't want to startle him back into silence. I trust him to tell me when he's ready, so I choose an equally important, but less intrusive, subject. "Why do you want the bite to be painful?"

He strokes his neck back and forth, eyes cast down. "Because I don't want to like it. It feels wrong."

My brows pull together, and I feel like I'm still missing a piece of the Leo puzzle. "Maybe you just don't want to like *me*?"

He ponders my hypothesis with his bottom lip tucked between his teeth, like he hasn't really looked at it this way before. "Perhaps."

I pick up his wrist gently and graze his pulse point. "Let it just be a bite, nothing more. I'm tired of hurting you."

"I'm—I'm not ready."

A sigh wheezes out of my lungs, but I nod and sink my teeth into him without taking away his pain.

I cannot help but imagine the alternative—if his eyes were set on me instead of glued to the corner of the room, his whole body ablaze with pleasure instead of pain—and let him go to bed with a pulse of anger and unquenched desire.

After switching off the light, I slip under the covers. The cool silk gown hugs my body, my nipples as hard as can be, the threads of the front corset rough to the touch. Leo's blood is still sweet in my mouth as I snake my hand down, curious to test the moves he taught me, but before it slips under the lace, a commotion echoes from the hallway.

The mindless giggles of King Pereira's drugged blood slaves scatter ice across my shoulders, and I grip the duvet. I hear them on the other side of my bedroom door, probably hanging from his arms as they did earlier, forced to suffer his every whim, and hold my breath.

"Step aside, boy. I need to see my bride," the old king slurs.

Alec's voice booms through the door, calm and perfectly collected. "The princess has already retired for the night, your grace."

"Let me in, you stupid fool. I'm marrying her tomorrow, and if you don't let me through, I'll make sure you visit the dungeons before you go."

I hide my face in my palms, my heart aching like it's being pricked by a thousand, icy needles.

"I can visit them tomorrow, *after* the wedding," Alec insists, like he's talking about something trivial like the weather. "Tonight, she's not to be disturbed, and my king would agree with me."

I scurry out of bed and wrap a thick robe around my frame, ready to flee if Pereira pushes his way through, but the nervous giggles of the blood slaves grow faint. Panting hard, I count to a hundred in my head, until all I can hear is the sound of my own agony, and press my forehead to the wooden door. What's one night of reprieve compared to a lifetime of misery? I should never have come here.

The doorknob is cold and heavy in my hand as I crack open the door and conjure a confidence I didn't even know I had, staring right into Alec's eyes. "He will punish you for that."

"He'll try." His lopsided grin reveals a dimple before he sobers up, his voice suddenly low and heavy. "It was worth it, though."

"Thank you," I croak.

Tomorrow will be wretched, but tonight, I'm still free.

Maybe one day makes all the difference. Maybe tomorrow, I'll have the strength to face it. It kills me that I've saved myself for a depraved, old man. I safeguarded my virginity for marriage like I was instructed to and will be condemned instead of rewarded for it.

I wonder if Lucas is a virgin, not sure I even know him at all.

Alec isn't.

I bet he's been with tons of women.

My gaze glides down his body, and my mind drifts.

He saved my life even though he hates me. He's loyal. Discreet. *And* he wants me.

I arch a decided brow. "What about you? Are you an idiot?"

"Am I a—" His throat bobs as the true meaning of my words passes between us.

"Once again, Mr. Beaumont... Are you an idiot?"

No arrogant smirk twists his handsome face. No witty comeback fills his breath—just an intense and grave look. "No."

I open the door wider, and he slips inside with feline grace. The current of energy between us changes, and my mouth dries up. Out there, I'm his princess. In here, who knows who's in charge?

His lips find mine, soft and warm, but tame, like he's wondering the same thing. Alec buries his knuckles deep in my thick mane and combs through the dark locks slowly, reverently, as though he always wondered how they would feel.

"Why did you accept?" I ask against his lips, breathless.

"Are you kidding? You're the ultimate forbidden fruit, princess." Honey and champagne fill my mouth as Alec holds the back of my neck and ravages me with his kiss, his tongue blunt and unapologetic. "And you deserve more than to marry this dreadful man," he says softly as he comes up for air.

I drum my fingers over his chest, taken aback by his candor. "You think I deserve you?" I ask in jest.

"You deserve *everything*." He kisses me again, and I mirror back every nibble and every lick, eager to stretch that second and third kiss into a long string of heated groans. I want to stroke to life the darkness in his eyes once more, the one he unmasked the night he carried me to safety from the second attack.

I want to scream *for* him—*with* him—and trace the angle of his jaw, down the slope of his neck to his chest. The wise-ass assassin stole many hearts at court, I bet, because every inch of him is shaped into a deadly weapon.

He hooks a finger in my front corset and tugs the threads loose one at a time, the repetitive motion incredibly erotic, and my breath catches when he grazes the swell of my sensitive breasts. I've never been naked in front of a male vampire before, let alone one that makes me feel as Alec does. I shimmy out of the silk, the periwinkle nightgown pooling at my feet.

A small hiss passes through Alec's tight lips, his hungry eyes drinking me in.

Cold air caresses my dark, pebbled nipples as I blurt out, "Shouldn't you get naked, too? This one-sided ogling contest unnerves me."

"You want me to get naked, Lucky?" He guides my hand to his belt with confidence, and I start unbuckling it with a smile.

"Are you going to answer every question with a question?"

He arches an equally playful brow. "Maybe. Why are you so tense?"

Intricate patterns swirl in the wood posters of the bed as I avert my gaze. "I was told I shouldn't expect to enjoy it. That it'll hurt."

"Christ! Stupid old fucks..." He frames my face with his hands and searches my eyes, his palms rugged and delicious on my cheeks. "I can't pretend to know if it'll hurt, but I'll make sure you enjoy it."

With that solemn promise, he licks my neck, his canines dangerously close to my jugular. For a moment, I wonder if he'll bite me, but he just slides his hands down and tests the feel of my breasts.

I cry out, more sensitive than I've ever been and jerk closer to him, wrapping my arms around his neck.

We kiss again, our movements more urgent as Alec teases the soft flesh, kneading it back and forth. "Fuck, you're so beautiful." He dips his head down and sucks one nipple inside his mouth, the sight of it almost obscene, and I sink my nails into his scalp, egging him on. The fire inside my belly swells higher with each brush of his tongue. I need *so much*, and yet he doesn't seem rushed.

"Come on," I say, tugging on his shirt.

With a gentle laugh, he peels it off before working the fabric into a ball and tossing it to the ground. I swallow hard, the planes of his bare chest coming into view. He's not special elite forces for nothing. Scars run across his left pectoral muscles, and a few more rush along his sides. The white lines create a patchwork of spiderwebs, the old wounds carved into his skin forever. I trace them with awe, and the hard muscles under my fingers steal my tongue.

Alec growls as I place a hot line of kisses from his abs to his neck. The sound echoes deep in my belly, and I nip his ear to hear it again.

The sinews of his large, powerful shoulders riddle me with lust as he snakes a hand down my stomach to the space between my legs, inching below the lace covering my sex. "Mmm. Feel how wet you are?"

"Yes. I need your fingers inside me now."

He arches a playful brow, falling to his knees in front of me. "I thought the Elders raised you in the dark about sex."

"They certainly tried."

His nails scrape my inner thighs as he glides my underwear down, and I glance down at him as I help him work the flimsy piece of lace past my feet.

His rough hands spread my legs, allowing him better access to my sex. "Then you should already know that you'll get even wetter after I've played with you a bit...and made you come. If it pleases your highness?"

"Yes," I answer, his arrogance and wicked smile riling me up.

A sweet kiss on my inner thigh causes my eyes to flutter as Alec draws sharp circles between my legs, faster than Leo did, until I'm panting.

A knot coils in my belly as I hiss. "By Nyx, don't stop."

He slides one finger inside me, then another, pressing hard against my pubic bone. So deep.

Knees buckling, I hold myself up to the wall. "Oh, Alec."

His tongue darts to the place where all my nerves collide, soft and teasing as his fingers harden on the inside, the sharp, relentless *rub, rub rub* driving me mad. I can't help but spread my legs wider, desperate for more of that delicious pressure as I grab a fist of brown curls.

A heady pleasure spreads across my belly and thighs, and the delicious sensation morphs into a throb as my inner walls clench around his fingers, the sweet pressure of his tongue almost painful now.

He withdraws and stands before serving me a slow, disarming kiss that leaves me wanton for more. His belt hits the floor with a forceful *slap*, and Alec finally drags off his pants, the black boxers underneath stretched by a huge bulge.

I sit on the edge of the mattress and reach for him. "Can I?"

His arms fall to his sides as he nods, his eyes as dark as the night.

Alec's hips jerk forward as I peel the fabric from him and wrap my hand around his length. Hard, but also soft in a way. And wet... I caress the tip. A bead of clear liquid glides across my thumb.

"Holy shit, Lucky."

My gaze darts up to meet his. "Does it feel good?"

"Yes."

"Why do you look angry?"

"Because I'm struggling to hold back. I really want to fuck you right now."

Pride and lust swell in my chest. "Tell me what you like."

I rub him up and down and up again, getting used to the feel of him. I don't think I could fit it all inside my mouth, but I wrap my lips over the tip, tasting him. Salt, sweat, and leather...I hum.

"Oh fuck. Ohh."

I take him deeper and move my head the way Evangeline did with Leo, using my tongue to suck and lick.

He grabs a fist of my hair to hold me off. "Enough."

I pout as he wrestles me off him. "I want to play with you more."

"Do you want me to fuck you or not?"

My throat bobs in anticipation. "Yes."

"Then let me concentrate for a sec." Leaving me alone and wanton on the bed, he searches the pockets of his discarded jacket and pulls out a plastic square. A condom, I realize, swallowing hard as he rolls it over himself.

Something about the sight liquefies my gut. I know he's right to put it on, and yet a rebellious part of me would prefer for Alec to be the father of my first child, and not the old drunk. Vampires can only conceive once a year, but the first few fertile cycles after the change can be all over the place. One might be coming up soon. Maybe that's why I've been thinking so much about sex. "What difference does it make? If I have to bear a child, let it be yours."

His garnet gaze holds mine captive, his voice breathless and vulnerable in a way it has never been. "I thought you hated me, Lucky."

"You're a choice. He's not. Do you have a family?" I'm not stupid. He might be married for all I know. Elite special forces do not get a lot of free time, but they are encouraged to procreate.

"No."

I exhale and search his gaze, hoping he's saying the truth and not just easing my conscience.

"It's just too risky." He slides the latex over his shaft and gently spreads my legs. "I'm going to tease you until you beg for more, and then I'm gonna fuck your brains out."

"Yes, please," I gasp.

He pushes two fingers inside me and strokes me with one hand, the other pinching my nipples in turn. Right when I'm on the cusp of falling over the edge, he stops and replaces his fingers with the tip of his hard length. "Are you ready?"

I bite my bottom lip. "Yes."

I feel a sting and a pressure. So much pressure, so much of him pushing inside...it's overwhelming, and my hips roll instinctively, taking him deeper. The stinging sensation relents almost immediately, my vampire healing powers probably to thank for the lack of pain.

"Are you okay?" he breathes on my neck.

I nod, and a hiccup quakes me. I'm actually doing this, having sex with Alec Beaumont... just the thought causes my eyes to roll inward, his cock tucked deep inside me even though it's forbidden. My lust for him rivals an equally delicious sense of pride. I made that decision for myself. I broke the rules, and it feels fucking incredible, way better than saving myself for a disgusting king.

A thrill lances up my spine, my body wrapped around him, the weight of him over me so foreign and exciting... I want more.

Alec moves slowly, and the delicious fire is back as he draws himself out only to push even deeper.

"Fuck." He cups my face, his fingers hard at the nape of my neck as he kisses me slowly, so delicately that I melt, the sensations powerful and new. Our bodies fused in more ways than one, and the friction of skin on skin sparks a fire in my gut. A wave of pleasure rolls through me, cresting higher and higher with each movement, unstoppable.

"Alec!" It's too much, and the throbbing sensation becomes a savage clench. "Yes! Don't stop."

Alec continues to thrust, one hand fastened over my mouth to muffle my screams as he kisses my neck softly. "Jesus, you're so hot when you come."

Blood pounds at my temples, the ecstasy coursing through my veins as I catch my breath. "Your turn, then."

A wide smile illuminates his face. "Aw... Lucky, I'm not done with you yet. We're not vampires for nothing. Unless you want to stop—"

"No!" I raise a brow. "What do you have in mind?"

"We're made for two things: violence and sex. Get on your knees, princess. I'm going to make you come in all the positions my dirty mind can think of, and trust me, that's a lot."

Lust blazes through my belly as I obey. By Nyx, I want him to teach me everything there is to know about sex and then some. I want him to use and defile my body until I'm not sure who I am anymore. "We only have tonight... We might as well make the best of it."

He nods, and the affirmation spurs us on even more, the rarity of a night like this not lost on us both.

Alec enters me from behind, our bodies perfectly made for all the wicked angles he has in mind, the orgasms coming quicker than they did at first as though Alec activated some type of secret mechanism inside me.

The rhythm increases, and he presses his forehead to my shoulder blade with a grunt. I twist around to face him again and wrap my thighs around his waist as I pull him back into me, eager to see his face as the pleasure rips through him. He looks so dark and focussed, his hips snapping into me with powerful thrusts, his abs straining at the effort. I drink in the sight of him as he stiffens on top of me and reaches his climax, his body melting on top of mine after a few seconds. "Oh... Princess. You've ruined me for all other women."

Other women...I nick his neck, staking my claim, before melting into his embrace. He's probably said that exact phrase to a million girls. This was a pity thing, after all, but I shake the ugly thought out of my head. Who cares why the handsome, royal assassin *fucked my brains out*. The important thing is that he did.

That I wanted him to do it.

That it was my choice.

Still... I'm taken by surprise at his tenderness, and how good his arms feel wrapped around me. "Stay."

He shifts me in his arms to stare into my eyes. "If I'm caught in your bed, they'll kill me."

"I understand."

My chest heaves in disappointment, but he tucks a loose strand of hair behind my ear. "No, I'll stay. I just had to hear myself say it out loud."

He strokes my arms up and down, the caress so sweet and intimate that my heart flips, and my stupid brain starts to plot impossible ways to keep him with me here, instead of saying goodbye. The different scenarios would probably end with him dead, but I can't help myself. I want him to stay.

And a tiny, intrusive voice in my head starts to contemplate Sebastian's suggestion. It's too late now for a public fuck, as he recommended, not without dire consequences, but I let myself wonder, for the first time, what would happen if I were to stand on that altar tomorrow, and say *no*.

CHAPTER 25

JEALOUS

ALEC

I'm in deep, deep shit. I thought I'd been in deep shit before, but this shit is worse. This is the shittiest shit of all.

I fucked Arielle Delacroix... and loved every second of it. My already big ego is bursting at the seams at the thought that I was the first inside her. The only. God, my dick throbs just thinking about it.

She stirs in my arms, and I slide a hand down her back to her perfect ass. With a gentle kiss at the nape of her neck, I rub down the length of her spine, caressing the flesh of her ass to her thighs and back a few times, until she gives me a high, needy whine. "You make a maddeningly nice big spoon."

"You want one last taste, Lucky?"

"Yes."

Thankfully, vampires heal too fast for her to be sore.

Tensing in anticipation, I adjust the angle of her hips and impale her on my cock. God. She's perfect. Tight and smooth and so deliciously out of my league.

Inside her, I feel more alive than I've felt in decades. This night wasn't supposed to happen, yet it somehow broke the streak of forgettable one-night-stands that governed my life. I want to worship her body until the point of exhaustion and start again tomorrow, but that's wishful thinking.

She moves with me, chasing her release, and I bring a hand to her front to caress her breasts, her nipples hard and sensitive. I fuck her slow and steady, the tip of my cock stretching her entrance with each thrust until she writhes.

"Harder."

I spread her open with a slow but forceful thrust, and her eyes roll inward as I tease her, hitting the same spot over and over again until she arches her back and moans, lost in the ecstasy of her orgasm for minutes, her walls soft and wet as her juices flow around my length, her mouth opened in a mix of surprise and joy.

"That was...amazing."

Vampires don't blush, but if we could, her cheeks would be crimson, and her wide, joyful grin tugs at a loose thread inside my heart.

"Are you really going to marry him?" The intrusive question worms its way out, crude and unexpected. I pushed it out of my mind all night, but I can't reign it in anymore.

She kisses my jaw. "Are you jealous, Mr. Beaumont?"

Fucking A.

I both hate and love how my surname rolls off her tongue. She's teasing me in both senses of the word, her pink tongue fucking with both me and my name in one go, making jokes like this is just another Tuesday.

She's about to marry a man she loathes. A proper princess would be crying her eyes out about the unfairness of her gold-ridden destiny, but not Arielle.

I shift on the bed, the sheet wrapped around my midriff. "You have options, you know. Say the word, and I'll sneak you out of here before the fuckers can blink and bring you back to Europe..."

"Ah! You're funny."

Her melodic laugh unravels me, and my eyes narrow. "I amuse you, now?"

"Yes."

I never understood these royals. Why is she not fighting this? Why would she marry this pig?

Her gaze collides with mine, ten times sharper than it was a second ago, sharp enough to cut through steel. "Is that what you did for Elle? You smuggled her out of the castle?"

My brows pull together.

"You lied to the king at the tribunal. I heard it, loud and clear."

My mind reels, thinking back on our earlier conversations. "You have powers, like your mother did."

The mention of her mother causes her eyes to glaze over, and she withdraws inside her royal carapace, the discussion coming to an abrupt stop. "My mother could bend people's will, and it got her killed." A minute passes in silence, Arielle retreating more and more into herself until she breathes, "Did you love her? Elle?"

I rub my chin, embarrassed. "I used to. Not anymore."

She nods to herself and holds the comforter to her chest, and I can't help but feel I said the wrong thing. Maybe she thinks that I've got a kink for royals, but that's simply not true.

"My brother will not let her be, you know."

"I know."

The first hints of dusk appear in the windows, and my stomach lurches. Her first-blood and his escort could appear at any moment to feed her before sundown.

Arielle angles her face away as I gather my clothes, straighten the collar of my shirt, and make sure my jacket is perfectly straight. "See you out there, Lucky."

Jude is standing guard on the other side of the door, both hands clasped in front of him. *Fuck.* We exchange a look, and his lips quirk before his serious, professional scowl returns. Jude is like a brother to me. He'd never sell me out, but I still would have preferred for this to remain my little secret.

I've lived for a hundred years, with many centuries to come, and yet this is probably the highlight of my life. How depressing. Despite the knot in my stomach and the dread in my heart, the midnight wedding is on track.

CHAPTER 26

KING OF ANGELS

LEO

"Dude, where were you?" Quentin asks from the other end of the hallway, scratching his neck. His dark hair is wet, so he's fresh out of the shower, and his neck is untouched.

I walk over to him. "I've had a servant trailing two steps behind me since we arrived, but he finally let me breathe."

First-bloods are trusted with most of the same responsibilities in this court, but my gender created a bit of an upheaval. While they can't keep me from the princess altogether, they made sure that a servant follows me everywhere on the guise of showing me the ropes.

"They don't like me here," I grunt.

Quentin's frown melts. "They don't like the fact that you're a dude. After the wedding, you should be in the clear. Come on, let's grab a bite, I'm starving." He pats my shoulder and guides me to the servant's hall.

Instead of secret passageways and intrigue, the common room feels and looks more like a cafeteria. A buffet is laid out by the kitchens with trays, plates, and utensils. Plants grow in white planters by the windows, crawling toward the last rays of twilight.

"Funny how vampires hate the sun, and yet, we're the ones stuck in the basement," I crack.

Quentin starts piling pastries on a plate. "I like it here. No moldy crypts and catacombs. And the view from the open-roof terrace is just—" he kisses his fingertips in approval.

It's a good thing he likes it, because Lucas won't return to Europe anytime soon. The princess either, I guess, though the mere thought of her marrying the sleazy king turns my stomach.

I slide a tray along the metal rail and peruse the options. "What about you? You look...full of blood."

Quentin's always a little pale in the evenings, right after feeding time.

"Lucas wasn't hungry. He looks nervous, to be honest. I don't think he likes the idea of the princess marrying his uncle."

Him and me both. I hated how the king looked at Arielle, like she was nothing but a meal.

Quentin and I sit with our breakfast at a 2-seat table, and he lowers his voice. "Is the king right to put you on a tight leash? Did the princess ask you to *do* her?"

"No," I answer immediately.

Quentin's got a big mouth, and he's a lousy liar, so I can't trust him to keep a secret. I shiver at what the king might do if he heard of my true feelings for Arielle. The soldiers here look about as *nice* as the ones in the Delacroix court—though the fact that Jasper Beaumont isn't among them is definitely a plus for Brazil.

"The king is a lucky fucker, that's for sure. I don't get why she agreed to marry him, though. I guess she wanted to be queen bad enough not to care about his age—or his looks."

I swallow a sour bite of omelet. "Don't say that."

"Sorry man. I just don't get it, honestly." He shrugs with his palms face up, and I feel like I'm the one being difficult when he's actually being an ass.

PRINCESS OF THORNS AND RUIN

"I don't think she had much choice on the matter," I finally snap.

He stuffs a big piece of bread in his mouth. "She's immortal and rich, and I'm sure she could kick that old king's ass if she wanted. Why would she go through with this wedding if she didn't want it?" His gaze flies to the entrance, and his eyes widen. "Is that your chaperone?"

I crane my neck around to check. "No, I'm in the clear. The princess is putting on her wedding dress."

A man leans casually on the juice bar, staring straight at us. Brown waves curl around his ears, and an ethereal light shines off the top of his head, almost like a halo.

I stiffen as our gazes meet, all the hair on my arms rising to attention. He licks his lips and raises his glass in greeting, his sky-blue irises fixed on me. My stomach cramps, and at once, I know I'm staring into the face of death.

Not just *any* death, but the one we ward ourselves against with crosses and hushed words.

I was raised on an island full of vampires, so I know what death wrapped in sin looks like, but this man is different. The skin at the base of my neck itches under his gaze, and my ears buzz, the laughter and conversations around us muffled by an echo.

One moment he's by the bar, and the next, he's a few feet away from us, his light swallowing everything else in the room. Maybe I blinked and missed his movement, but I doubt it, and I'm left in a haze, unable to stop staring.

"Hello."

When death says hello, you either grin and bury your soles in the ground, or turn around to run.

A smile tugs at the corner of my lips, because I prayed for this. Now that he's here, I don't want it, but I can't pretend I haven't yearned for it.

"Who are you?" Quentin asks. "How did you move so fast?"

"Leave us," the man dismisses my colleague with a curt nod.

Quentin grips the side of his plate but obeys, not even meeting my gaze as he flees, probably under the same thrall as I am.

The stranger takes his place and tilts his head to the side, surveilling me the way you do a child or a puzzle. He sets his glass in front of him and runs a finger along the rim.

"You're...afraid. Why?" He says with a brash, unfamiliar accent.

My heart hammers in my chest, the rise in adrenaline now prompting me to jump to my feet and run, but I know better than to turn my back on a predator.

He inches closer, and I'm floating on air. The sense of...peace is overwhelming, like a shroud has been laid over my shoulders, my heart, my fucking *soul*. "Are you here to kill me?" I ask.

He leans in ever so slightly and squints, his eyes set on me like he can see directly into my soul. "Why would ye say that?"

That's a yes.

"Do you wish to harm the princess?"

"I would never hurt her." The stranger kneels next to me. "Can I confide in you, Leo Callas?" The demon cups the side of my face, his thrall so potent, I can't move. "I was hired by Felipe Pereira for a... disagreeable task."

His breath caresses my lips, heavy with the promise of a damned, unescapable kiss. His presence fills my blood with something foreign, a lust the likes of which I've never felt. I *crave* the peace he incites in me, and my blood sings like a fucking choir under his thrall.

"What are you doing to me?" The question costs me all the air left in my lungs, my soul crying out for him, for his kiss, his bite, and the sweet, sweet death he's so clearly offering.

He scrapes my wrist with his teeth, right where Arielle bit me last, and licks the scar. "I'll tell you what I was hired to do, and you'll let me speak with the princess."

Blood rushes at my temples, my will as brittle as his touch. "She's getting fitted in her wedding dress."

"All the more reason to hurry."

CHAPTER 27
WEDDING BELLS
ARIELLE

T he living room next to the balcony has been reorganized to serve as a dressing room for the wedding, allowing for Bella, the hairdresser, and the make-up artist to tend to my beauty needs, but no amount of face paint could cover up the claustrophobic ache in my heart. Victor might have made a power match for himself... but it doesn't mean I need to do the same.

But it's my duty. To my kingdom, my people. My mother's legacy.

White birds fly in the pink sky, the bright hues of twilight acting as a physical timer, counting down the minutes until I have to walk down the aisle. Orange was safe, pink is alarming, and the deep purple streaks mean it's almost time.

As my stylist adjusts the endless string of buttons that run down my arms, my fingers start to shake.

"Let's take ten." She claps her hands, forcing the Pereira-employed staff out, and whistles out after them.

I inch forward to sit on the oval ottoman, the long, laced train of the dress weighing me down, the delicate fabric ready to rip at the first sign of a swift movement.

Alec slips inside the room from the same door Bella just exited, stealthy as a ghost. I meet his golden stare in the mirror, and my chest shrinks as the air inside the room is suddenly ten degrees colder.

He drills holes into the back of my white dress with his eyes, the effect as tangible as a graze of his fingers. "My offer still stands. You just have to say the word."

The tight corset barely allows me to breathe. "Am I so lucky now, Mr. Beaumont?"

"Why are you going along with this marriage?" His voice is quieter than I thought possible, but his lips moved, so I know I didn't just read his thoughts.

I spin around to face him. "It's my duty. When I'm queen, I might be able to steer this court toward reform." I bite my lips, knowing I sound naive at best considering all that we saw last night. "If not now, then after the king's death... Upholding the laws of Hatten is my family's sacred responsibility."

Alec's phone buzzes in his pocket, but he quickly turns it off. "Your family... Don't get me wrong, Lucky, but vampires, especially kings, are all violent and greedy. Your family makes no exception."

"Victor is a good man," I say, more as a knee-jerk reaction than true conviction. After all that happened in France, I'm not sure I even know my brother at all. "If we don't change this court, we're all doomed."

Alec paces the room, shaking his head. "Victor might be good in the sense that he doesn't torture people for pleasure, but he's about as good at hiding his real appetites as my younger brother is. If he cared so much about our laws, he'd start by reforming his own court."

"What in the name of Nyx do you mean?" I crane my neck around to follow his movements and pat down the soft, white silk covering my stomach, his words stroking a chord inside me.

Alec squints the same way he did when I asked him to stay the night with me, as though he doesn't fully trust me. "You really don't know?"

I shake my head, afraid I'll shatter if I speak too loud or move too fast, feeling like the rose from the fairytale, suspended inside a glass jar for the rest of time, condemned to wither one petal at a time.

"The king might be married to Adele Chastain, but he prefers his blood slaves—and his lovers—to be male. He might have gone through with the arranged marriage your brother imposed, but everyone knows it's all for show. A ploy to produce heirs. Peter Chastain is so obsessed with his legacy, I'm surprised he didn't convince your brother to marry you to his son."

It shouldn't surprise me considering how Victor tried to vaguely allude to a possible affair with Lucas, but my face wrinkles. "I don't get it. Why would Adele marry him, then? He wasn't supposed to become king, so she could have married someone else."

"For the same reason you're about to marry Felipe Pereira. For duty. Adele gets first-pick at the blood slaves and keeps a handful of lovers in return. Only...Pereira will not let you do as you please. He won't allow you this sort of freedom." He curses under his breath as his phone starts buzzing again and glances at the screen only to bury it back inside his jacket. "As soon as Felipe dies, I expect you'll be pushed aside in favor of his oldest son. Victor *knows* this. If he said otherwise, he's been lying to you."

All my life, I've been taught that our power depends on alliances, and that queens can be as powerful as their husbands. Like so many things about my education, it was a diluted, sugary version of the truth. I've been fooled by Victor. He sold me on the idea of reform, dangling in front of me the possibility that I'd be queen for centuries after Felipe's death.

My blood ices at the thought that my brother never breathed a word of the alternative to me, probably hoping I'd remain dutiful and stupid long enough for him to get his way. I grip my throat, the pressure there almost unbearable as I hold in a scream.

"I answer only to you. What do you want me to do?" Alec asks, his quiet tone begging me to make the right decision.

A lost piece of me clicks into place. I don't have to go through with this and let others dictate my life to fulfill some sort of duty, or to please people.

I'm a Delacroix.

A princess.

A woman.

A demon.

"Get me out of here." I open my mouth to speak further, but a knock at the door startles us both.

Leo enters the room through the servant's door and walks over to me, his face ashen, and leans to my ear. "The angel wants to speak to you."

"Now?" Alec barks.

"I think you should hear him out." Leo doubles-back to open the door for the Celt.

Keenan's short brown curls and glacial-blue eyes look even more angelic than last night, the glow of his skin mesmerizing. "Your highness, I was hired to make sure you'd go through with the wedding and kill you if you didn't." He shoots a sideways glance to my first-blood. "And Felipe asked me to get rid of Leo during the ceremony."

"Why hire you? Pereira's got an army of vampires," Alec dead-pans.

Keenan holds his deadly gaze without a hint of shame. "They were superstitious. They thought a curse was sure to befall any vampire who raised a hand on Katharina Delacroix's daughter."

My mother's name brings tears to my eyes. "Why are you telling us?"

"What can I say? I'm a sucker for beautiful girls, and though I bargained a hefty price, I don't like his manners."

Alec reaches inside the pocket of his jacket and unveils a long, aconite-coated blade, the scent masked by his cologne but present all the same. "Cut the bullshit and tell us the whole truth."

Keenan purses his lips to one side, his eyes wrinkled like he's about to smile. "Yer first-blood has what it takes to be one of mine.

It's a rare thing to find a mortal compatible with my special strain of disease. Felipe wants him dead, and for that, I cannot stand."

"I don't want to be like you," Leo growls.

"Ye've got years to change your mind. I won't let some old fart King deprive ye of them. Not if I can help it." He lifts his chin in my direction. "And that necklace is actually cursed. Once you take your vows, the spell will activate, and you'll have to obey Felipe Pereira's every command."

A violent chill takes a hold of me. "I—I can't take it off." The clasp seems to be stuck, and Alec swears as he tries and fails to snap it off my neck.

Tears flood my eyes, and I hold out an arm for Alec to stop. I need a minute to think. If the necklace is cursed, maybe a spell now prevents us from opening the clasp. The repetitive buzzing sound coming from Alec's phone echo through the room as I draw in a slow breath.

My lover finally digs his phone from his pocket and brings it to his ear. "What?" he barks, stepping closer to the balcony.

"I need to speak with the princess. Let me in," Lucas says loudly from the hallway, probably met with resistance by Alec's second-in-command, Jude. "Ari... Come on, it's important," my ex-best-friend whines through the closed door.

No. No Ari, not after the way he treated me yesterday.

I school my face into a mask of boredom not to give my true intentions away and crack open the door. "I am your princess, soon to be your queen, Lord Pereira, and you will address me as such."

"As you wish, your Majesty." Lucas' face is a graveyard, his skin so white, I almost don't recognize him. "Something is happening. Nobody will tell me anything, but everyone is acting weird."

I grip the chain around my neck. "What's happening is that your uncle plans to enslave me with this wretched thing."

Alec joins me by the door. He brings a hand to his mouth, and his edges shimmer like he's shaking too fast for my eyes to see. "Jude. Please let Lord Pereira inside."

Jude pushes Lucas inside the room and closes the door behind them.

"Your highness, it was Sebastian Chastain on the phone. Your brother, Victor, was just killed," Alec croaks. "He was ambushed at the airfield."

I stand, shocked, my blood pounding like a drum at my temples. If Victor is dead, that means...

My lover bends the knee. "Long live the Dark Queen."

ARIELLE'S STORY continues in Queen of Ashes and Scars.

Pre-order now.

Who's Eleanor Delacroix? What happened to her? Read the **prequel** now (with an appearance from your favorite bodyguard, **Alec Beaumont!**) **Free on KU!**

LOVELY READERS

To support me and the books, please leave a rating or a review on Amazon.

To keep up with my releases and receive exclusive extras, including bonus epilogues and special sneak peeks, join my newsletter.

Click here: http://bit.ly/anyaslair

Xoxo, Anya.

Connect with me on Facebook: https://www.facebook.com/AnyaJCosgrove/

Take a sneak peak at the prequel, Magnetic, after this.

MAGNETIC: THRONE OF SHADOWS PREQUEL

Free on KU!

Who said life was a fairy tale? Because I'd gladly slice that jerk's head off.

I'm Vicky, though that's not really my name. Lying becomes second nature when you're on the run.

I never expected to end up half-naked in the woods. I didn't plan to stumble upon the most powerful shifter clan in North America and three of the sexiest men I've ever laid eyes on.

Dominic, the fun and reckless new wolf.

Sam, the hot doctor with glacial-blue eyes.

And Gabriel, the intense, secretive alpha who wants nothing to do with me.

My real name is a one-way ticket back to hell, and my secrets need to stay dead and buried like the girl I used to be.

Sleeping Beauty, Snow White, Red Riding Hood—I can be all three. I can use my powers to earn a place in their werewolf town, away from the bite of my past mistakes. I can use them—and their bodies—to survive.

The only thing I can't do is fall for them.

Magnetic is a stand-alone, steamy reverse harem romance featuring a kick-ass heroine and three swoon-worthy werewolves. Pick up your copy now!

MAGNETIC SNEAK PEEK - KISS WITH A FIST

Vicky

A girl needs a lot of sugar to heal her broken heart.

"Large chocolate caramel mochaccino, extra-extra foam, please," I say, searching my skirt's pocket for a ten dollar bill. Organic, eco-friendly sugar is expensive.

There's no line behind me, so the barista is in no hurry. She gawks at my shimmering braid as she prepares my getting-over-a-guy drink, pouring a bit of foam to the side. The misplaced bubbles splash to the counter, but she's too busy checking me out to notice. A big blackboard towers behind her, her fingers white with chalk. When a trickle of caramel sauce splatters on her flats, she curses, finally looking away.

Even when I'm muted, humans react to my lure. Her hazel pupils are dilated, and her chest is flushed. Usually, it'd give me a boost of confidence, but not today.

She leans closer and hands me the plastic cup. "Here you go." Sweat and coffee beans tickle my nose, the slightest hint of arousal lurking behind them. Her gaze darts to my ass.

"Thank you." I grab my drink and avoid touching her hand, sparing her the mind-numbing horniness that would follow if our fingers were to brush.

I slurp my coffee and sit on a stool, my shoulders hunched. The spring in my step is missing; I should offer a reward for its return.

Getting dumped sucks. Sex demons don't get dumped. It just doesn't happen. Vandellas never get dumped. We tire out our prey and move on. Being cast aside by my favorite lover and his brother in the same summer just blows. Why do Walker men care about monogamy, anyway? It's so overrated.

If my succubus friends knew about this... It's so humiliating.

A guy stops next to me, and I glance up from my drink.

"Hey," he says, his eyes lingering on the scruffy hem of denim at my mid-thigh.

He's got blond hair, a chiseled jaw, and nice strong shoulders. He's super hot, but I don't care. Me, the girl who feeds on sex.

"Hey," I answer half-heartedly.

"You're not from around here, are you?"

I snort. "No, I'm not."

I'm thousands of miles away from where I was born, with no intention to ever return. No wonder I don't fit in with Americans—or humans in general.

"I'm Jace." He extends his hand, and the edge of a tattoo peeks from under his sleeve.

I bat my eyelashes without touching him. "Hi, Jace. I'm Vicky, and normally I'd do you, but I'm having a real bad day."

His eyes are wide at my brazenness.

I get that a lot. It's hard to be proper when you know all the dirty desires and wicked fantasies people hide beneath layers of denial. I might not be a witch, but I sure can read human emotions better than most. Between the blood rushing to his ears and the abrupt bob of his Adam's apple, I'm pretty sure Jace is confused by his raging erection.

I wave my hand for him to leave, and he staggers to the cash register, adjusting his pants.

Still... I'm hungry. Vandellas need to feed almost every day. It doesn't have to be the whole nine yards, but sexual energy is my chicken, rice and carrots. A great kiss is like munching on a bag of chips. Second base is French fries and a Coke. A good sensual massage equates to a nice healthy salad.

Human sex packs enough calories for a day. Good demon action is the dirtiest of feasts and keeps me going for thirty-so hours, forty when I'm really into the guy.

And I also need food and water, so it's no wonder I don't have time to save the world or get a real job.

The worst part about my day is that I got dumped *before* sex. I never expected my latest fling to last long—the man was a boy scout at heart, but he couldn't even do the guy thing and wait until *after* we fucked to break the news, and I have to eat today.

Bag of chips it is. In three strides, I've caught up with Jace. Before he can say anything, I grip his collar and plant my lips on his. The mint tucked behind his teeth clashes with the taste of coffee, but I soldier through, his mouth hot and pliant against mine. He encircles my waist, desire surging through him. A low moan rumbles at the back of his throat, and he whimpers when I pull away.

"Nice kiss, Jace. I'd recommend you to a friend." I wink and turn on my heels.

Humans generally take minutes to rationalize what happened.

I steal kisses, but never sex. Sex needs to be fun for both parties, and I'm not about to force myself on a human. Sure, I give them a nice sample of what I'm offering, but I always, always mute myself and give them a chance to say no. Few men ever say no.

Still. I'm tired. Men are too predictable, and the ones that aren't prefer to chase after girls that keep them waiting. Playing hard to get isn't my forte.

Demons are mostly the same. They fight to upstage one another for the honor of being my favorite conquest. They're self-conscious of their performance, hoping their stamina will be praised to future generations. My ex was different.

Tears mist over my eyes, but I will them away. We didn't work, so I'm glad he found something real.

I could kill the bitch.

A relentless sun scorches the recently paved parking lot, the black asphalt shimmering. I shrug off my jacket and wipe sweat off my forehead with the sleeves. My frilly top is tied right below my breasts, leaving my stomach bare, and a gentle breeze coming from the trees at the back of the lot cools me down.

Raised voices become more and more audible as I near the green Jeep I stole earlier. A teenage girl wearing a barista uniform is arguing with a man with squared shoulders and a cheap tattoo.

"Come on, baby, you can't keep torturing me like this." The man grabs her arm a little too strongly for my taste, and I pause. He looks older than her by at least ten years.

"I have to go to work," she says, fleeing from his grasp. She walks around a big wood bench towards the employee's back door.

He stops her a few feet short from her goal and pins her to the wall. "I'll get you at nine. We can go to my place. I'll show you a good time, babe."

Her mouth curls down. "I told you. I'm not ready for any of that yet. Brianna is picking me up."

His cajoling tones vanishes. "You're no virgin, so what's the problem? Scared to handle a real man?" He pinches her ass and hikes her skirt up.

The girl shoves his hand off her, but he steps between her legs.

When he crushes his mouth to hers, I leap in their direction. "Hey!"

"Mind your own business—" The wannabe rapist stops, his jaw slack. They were both too busy to notice me before, but now I've got their attention.

I put my jacket down on the bench and take a deep breath. "Do you need help?"

The girl nods.

"Oh, I do need help, sweetheart." The disgusting perv licks his lips and lets go of the girl, prowling toward me.

I'm made to seduce men, but I can also scare the crap out of them and break their noses when the situation demands it. My fist splits his face in two before I can form a thought, and I shake out my hand, jolts of pain radiating across my knuckles. The bastard had strong bones.

With a gasp, the girl covers her face with her hands.

"What the fuck?" He gurgles, and blood sprays everywhere.

Gripping his greasy hair, I angle his ear to my mouth. "You'll leave that girl alone. You'll go home, shave your disgusting beard, and reflect on how you became such a loser." The compulsion dilates his pupils. Humans are so easy to manipulate.

He bolts off without a word, and I eye my damsel in distress with suspicion. I've run into situations like these where the girl gave me hell for saving her ass. *Love* is a funny thing.

"Thank you." She tucks a strand of hair behind her ear, her cheeks red.

I dust off my jacket and hook it around my elbow. "You're welcome."

"How did you—"

"Krav Maga. Google it." I glance at her name tag. "He won't bother you anymore if you don't go looking for him. Older guys are sexy, I get it, but he's sleazy." Our gazes lock, and I crank up my powers. The demonic haze ought to make a lasting impression on her. "Stay away from creeps, Heather." I stomp off, satisfied by my good deed.

MAGNETIC SNEAK PEEK
- FIGHTER

Vicky

My journey to California takes me deep into the heart of Middle America, and I spend a few days under the Texan sun, sampling sexy cowboys. My last stop is Arizona where a few friends of mine have set up shop.

Two vandellas I've known for years own a fusion cuisine place in Phoenix, and they're the exact company I need right now: fun and uncomplicated. Our powers don't work on each other, so I can actually relax in the presence of my own kind and know they're not secretly chatting with me so I'll fuck them later.

As soon as I step into Isabel's restaurant, my stomach lurches. The homey atmosphere has been replaced by a smothering silence. Nobody is chatting at the tables or raising their glasses in cheer, the place emptier than my ex-husband's heart. The red curtains are closed, and the feeble sunshine filtering through the sheer fabric twinkles against airborne lint particles.

"Isabel?" I call out, the hairs on the nape of my neck rising in time with the puffs of dust under my feet. I'm clearly the first customer to come through the doors in weeks.

"Vicky?" Isabel's voice is quiet, a stark contrast to her usual joyful tone. She appears from the revolving kitchen door and stops when she sees me. Her long black hair is tied in an untidy bun behind her head, her red-rimmed eyes wet with unshed tears.

I step closer to my friend. "What's going on?"

Her gaze darts to the floor. "It's Cora. She's missing." Cora's her twin sister, and they are inseparable.

"Oh, no! How long—"

She sniffles. "Three weeks."

I'm not sure that the twins have spent more than half a day apart since they were born, and my throat tightens. "Do you know who did it?"

"I have an idea..." She fumbles in her jacket's pocket for a tissue and presses a few buttons on her cell.

I squeeze her shoulder. "I'll help you get her back."

"Thank you. Tea?"

"Sure." She ushers me into her adjoined apartment behind the kitchen and motions for me to sit at one of the white textured chairs by the glossy quartz island. The electric kettle wheezes as she plugs it into the outlet. A few spoonful of Oolong Tea are dumped in a terracotta teapot. Isabel is still crying, sniffling into a Kleenex, and I give her some time to breathe.

We wait a few minutes for the tea to infuse, and she serves us both a cup.

I blow on the steaming beverage. "Tell me everything. Was it one of her regulars? Was it a demon?" Vandellas are sought-after mates, and it's not that unusual for a lovelorn ex or a jealous lover to try to enslave us into submission. Mind-blowing sex and craziness often go together. "I know people. They could do a spell and locate Cora quickly if you gave me some of your blood. You are identical twins, so your blood has got to be the same as hers, right?"

Isabel turns green, and her hands shake. "Listen, Vicky... it wasn't a regular. It was vampires..."

A loud engine roars onto the street in front of restaurant.

My friend plays nervously with her necklace. "I'm so sorry."

A flurry of muffled footsteps echoes in my sensitive ears, and my blood turns to ice in my veins. Vampires... as in the creatures that have been hunting me. "You sold me out." An anchor of disappointment sinks in my chest, dragging down the last shred of trust I nurtured toward the universal laws of friendship and decency.

A loud cry dribbles from Isabel's guilty lips. "It's not just Cora. They've been raiding every vandella-owned establishment looking for you. They took one girl from each family and vowed to keep them hostage until you were surrendered to them. V, I'm so, so sorry."

"Not sorry enough, clearly," I say, kicking off my beautiful, peep-toe Valentino pumps.

I do the only thing a demon can do in this situation. I run. For a five-foot-four woman, I'm a hell of a runner. I slam the back door open, the tall apartment buildings towering from above. The trash and recycling bins clank together as I bump them with my elbow.

The smell of rotten fish clogs my nose. Two leather-clad, male vamps are blocking the exits on each side of the alley, and I stop. My bare feet dig into the gravel. A fire-escape ladder hangs from a balcony about twelve feet above me, and I jump with my hands stretched above my head. A proud grin curls my lips as my knuckles turn white against the base of the ladder, and I scurry upwards. The rusty bars are slippery as fuck, a thin film of rain from this morning's storm still licking the metal.

The vampires follow, their weight pulling the ladder down.

I kick the one directly below me in the forehead, and he grunts when his back collides with the ground. The second one stays out of reach, and I climb until I'm at the top of the building, my lungs and knees hurting.

The roof is square and barren. I run to the opposite edge and peer over it. Vampires patrol the street in front of the restaurant, holding a few passersby at bay, their fake police cars the perfect explanation for this manhunt. My chest heaves. I count eight bloodsuckers in total and scan their bare arms for the Delacroix's mark, but none of them seems to bear the tattoo. They probably belong to another family. I bet Ludovic called in a few favors to see me home quickly.

The closest building is a stretch too far, but it's the only possible escape. If I manage to jump on the neighbor's roof, I'll have a clear way down the street and might be able to disappear into the crowded boulevard. The first vampire spills onto the roof from the way I came.

I crouch, my toes planted firmly in the ground, and consider the height of the ledge. I'll have to pick up speed, use the ledge as a stepping stone, and jump. There's no time to aim for anything particular; I'll just hope for the best.

I leap into action, pushing myself, and dive feet first from the tall roof. I hang in midair for a moment, my gaze searching for a safe place to land, but the ground is coming way too fast, and the building is still too far away. A bad whiplash slices through my neck as my fingers finally grasp a railing, my head flying backwards. Dangling off the neighbor's alcove windowsill, I grit my teeth. My muscles scream from the abuse, and I need a moment to recover from my bad jump.

A vampire is perched on the balcony two stories below me.

He was bitten young, at sixteen or seventeen, and he's handsome, his spiky hair perfectly gelled. A loud grunt escapes him, and he flings himself a story higher, his long arms now barely six feet away from my ankles.

He shoots me an impressed smile. "I didn't think you'd make that jump."

"You and me both, Twilight." I exhale and start climbing, heading for the nearest balcony. A cold hand closes around my leg, and the weight of my pursuer stops my ascension. Twilight crawls over me like a vine. Damn vampire stamina. His arm encircles my waist, and I let go, hanging from his grasp like a very annoyed Barbie doll. Two others come to his aid, climbing the wall. Their black arms and legs remind me of spiders scurrying up their nets to collect their bounty.

The three vamps slowly lower me to the ground, passing me around as though we're *Cirque du Soleil* acrobats. I scratch one eye, kick one pair of balls and bite a neck on my way down, but it doesn't seem to bother them enough to drop me. There's now about a dozen vamps in police uniforms waiting below, and I know I've lost this round.

Once my feet hit the asphalt, they tie my hands behind my back with zip ties. Twilight presses hard on my jaw and forces a red liquid down my throat. The jasmine taste is unmistakable, so I know it's a sleep potion. He snaps a picture of me with his phone before they throw me in the back of a huge armored, red-striped SUV.

PINKISH CLOUDS STRETCH towards a deep blue sky when I wake up in the back seat of a moving car. I'm lying down on the leather, my head bumping against the door every few seconds. The scenery blurs beyond the windows, the highway flanked by high trees. Twilight is typing on his phone at my feet, and the driver is arguing over who gets to choose the music with the vamp sitting next to him.

A smirk glazes my lips.

Three vampires and a conscious vandella locked in a car... They clearly haven't dealt with my kind before. I'm baffled that they didn't fly me over to Europe immediately. Maybe they wanted to set up some kind of exchange. Moving slowly, I test the strength of my restraints, but they're pretty solid. Bummer.

The movement catches Twilight's attention, and I bat my eyelashes at him. "Nice moves out there."

He braces his hands against the back of his neck, his arms stretched on each side, his muscles bulging inside his leather jacket. My short, black dress is hiked up almost to my waist, and I catch him stealing a glance at my lace panties. *Piece of cake.*

I slide my bare foot up his thigh, and he sucks in air. "You know what I am, don't you?" I drawl, whipping my powers up into a frenzied wave and letting it wash over him. His length hardens immediately beneath my toes.

"Yes," he breathes.

"If you let me go, I'll be very grateful."

The front passenger cranes his neck around. "Don't chat with her. Give her another dose."

My prey fumbles with his jacket's inside pockets. I press on his crotch. He drops a small vial that bounces off his knee and disappears beneath the driver seat. Instead of reaching for the potion, Twilight leans closer, lust dilating his pupils and making his red eyes a shade warmer.

"You want to kiss me, don't you?" I sit and stretch toward him. "It's better than you can imagine."

"Stop, Ian! *Stop right now*," the driver screams.

Ian moans as I glide my tongue across his bottom lip, and just like that, I've won. *Thank you very much.*

I drink his energy in, ravaging his mouth and recharging my batteries. "Untie me, Twilight."

He frees me, spellbound. I discard the zip tie, elbow him right in the nose and snap his neck. That won't kill him, but it'll buy me time. I can't quite behead him with my bare fingers.

The car swerves, and the other two try to get a hold of me, their arms clawing at emptiness. One finger hooks itself in the fabric of my dress, ripping a few buttons open. They both freeze. My breasts are a killer asset. The passenger is too busy ogling them to prevent me from punching him square in the nose. He cries out in pain, his hands flying to his damaged bones.

I wrap my arm around the driver's neck from behind. "Pull over."

His hands clench around the steering wheel. "No."

I hop in his lap and try to push down the brakes.

The car flies off the road, our bodies hanging in mid-air for a moment before we all tumble around the cabin. My skull cracks the windshield, a humongous headache slicing through me. The screech of metal booms through my ears, and we land upside-down in the ditch.

Dizzy, I pat my head, my fingers digging into a mess of tangled locks. Glass shards bite into my ass as I sit up. The driver's got a huge piece of sunroof embedded in his neck, a red wave gushing from the wound. He shuffles around, and a sharp pain thunders inside my stomach. I let out a strangled shriek and look down.

The fucker impaled me on a silver dirk. I yank it out of me and slice his head off. His body explodes in a cloud of dust, leaving only a clump of clothes behind, and I cough his acidic leftovers out of my lungs. The passenger's head was bashed in by the glove compartment, but I cut his throat, too. Good beheading techniques are key to a worry-free life.

Twilight is nowhere to be found. He might have been ejected through a window or dusted by the accident. I exhale, pushing the stinging pain to the corners of my mind. Ashes soil my hand when I pat down the driver's clothes for a phone. A victorious grunt escapes me when I grip my stolen cell, but a weird crackling sound prevents me from dialing.

A loud boom at the front of the car is followed by an orange flash of light visible through the windshield. The smell of melting wires pervades the air, and I crawl out as fast as I can through a broken window, the engine fire heating up my arms.

Tall pines dance before my woozy vision when I finally manage to stand, the trees knitted so close together that they blur into a green and brown blotch. Hands shaking, I press on my belly and dial Liam's number. Calling my ex for help was *so* not on my list of things to do today, but shit happens. Lately, shit happens to me a lot more than it happens to other people.

My brows furrow at the absence of the ringing sound. No reception. Great.

Black smoke burns my lungs, so I walk away from the fire. Flames are slowly creeping toward the console, and with my luck, the whole thing is going to explode soon.

The chill of the night bites into my feverish skin. My bloody fingers cramp around the surviving buttons of my dress as I pop them into place. When I'm half-decent, half-roadkill, I slump to my butt in the squishy leaves littering the bottom of the trench.

The slope leading back to the road is too steep for my stab wound, and I wait for the sound of passing cars to keep me company and give me hope. Maybe someone will see the fire and rescue me. My lure sparks, creating a glitchy glimmer over my skin. The demonic survival-mode is kicking in. I could really use a kiss right now to boost my healing abilities, but there's no warm body available. Nothing but suffocating flames dancing to an ominous cricket choir.

The moon rises high in the sky, but there's still no cars. No knight in shining armor to respond to my lust beacon and feed me his energy—and his lips. Shadows lurk at the edge of my vision. I'm either going to bleed out, or I'll survive the wounds only to succumb to hunger in the middle of the woods.

Ain't that a stupid way to die.

CONTINUE READING. HTTP://BIT.LY/READMAGNETIC

SHADOW WALKER

Read the series that started it all! Fall for the shadows. Kiss the enemy.

Nothing stays black and white in a world full of shadows...

I'm Alana Mitchell, and for my twentieth birthday, I got a brand-new magical destiny instead of the laptop I was saving for.

I'm a witch. I have powers I can't control, enemies I know nothing about, and a legacy I can't begin to grasp.

There's a shadow-world out there waiting to swallow me whole, a world I didn't even know existed until I used my magic and unleashed hell upon my naïve self. From heart-eating ghouls to glamors, potions, and spells... nothing is as it seems.

A renegade demon and his brother are teaching me the ropes and driving me crazy with their I-know-better attitudes, beckoning stares and stupidly handsome faces.

At this rate, I'll flunk Witchcraft 101. I want to hunt down the bastards that destroyed my future, but the brothers' past is threatening to steal my soul and tear me apart—literally.

To survive, I must embrace the darkness simmering inside me and unleash the devil within, no matter the consequences...

PICK UP YOUR COPY NOW!
http://bit.ly/buyshadowwalker